REMEMBER MY NAME

LAURENCIA HOFFMAN

ENCOMPASS INK

Published by Encompass Ink

Edited by Sarah Brandon

Cover Design by Melissa Stevens at The Illustrated Author Design Services

CONTENTS

For Timothée Chalamet, who inspires me endlessly.

1

There was a new restaurant in town. It was too fancy for Shane's taste, but his friend Troy *had* to try the place.

Heaving an exasperated sigh, he stood in the waiting area and listened to the cheesy music. It was just like Troy to be late, leaving Shane to fend for himself in a crowded and uncomfortable area. Troy was lucky they were best friends, otherwise, he'd be getting a lot of shit for it.

He kept checking his phone, trying to appear busy since some of the patrons were shooting him dirty looks. Shane didn't own just-in-case clothes, so he didn't have anything appropriate to wear to a restaurant like this. If he had known, he would have borrowed something from Troy.

Most of the time, Shane didn't care about how he looked. It wasn't that he was lazy or didn't try, but he didn't want to carter to the judgments of other people. His comfort was the most important thing.

His eyes flicked upward to settle on a familiar face. He could have sworn that his eyes were playing tricks on him, yet, when he blinked and returned his gaze to the tall, hand-some blond, he was still there.

The blond was laughing and patting one of his friends on the back. Shane didn't recognize the people he was with.

For a moment, he was frozen. This seemed like a dream, a nightmare, or a hallucination – anything but reality.

And then those sparkling blue hues spotted him, and the blond's face turned white as a ghost.

"Shane," he whispered.

Lifting his chin, he looked the man up and down as if he had only just noticed him. "The one and only. How long have you been back, shithead?"

The man's cheeks flushed pink and he excused himself from his group of friends. As he took a step closer to Shane, Shane took a step back.

"Just a couple of weeks. I'm here for work."

"Of course you are. I'm not sentimental enough to think that you'd be here for me." Running his tongue along the front of his teeth, Shane folded his arms.

The older man swallowed hard. "Do you think we could talk outside?"

"Oh, sure. Wouldn't want your friends to think I ever meant something to you, right?"

The blond gave him a stern look. "That's not fair."

Heaving a sigh, he obliged the man by exiting the restaurant and standing to the side of the entrance.

"What the fuck do you want to talk about, Callan? How you broke my heart and abandoned me, forever tainting my view of love?"

"Did I really?" With a sigh, Callan shook his head. "I thought you might have forgotten me by now."

"Unfortunately for the both of us, I didn't." He wanted to say so much more, like how the six months they had spent together had changed his life. But he didn't want to give Callan the satisfaction of knowing just how deeply he'd been affected by their relationship. "What's with the entourage?"

His features brightened. "They're my colleagues, actually. I'm sure you remember my love of photography."

"How could I forget?"

"Well, I'm dabbling in journalism now. And I'm able to provide my own pictures."

"Good for you." He wanted to grumble something about how he'd never doubted Callan, but thought better of it. "What are you working on?"

"Just a piece about some of my favorite places." He paused. "I could include you if you want."

Shane's first instinct was to say yes. Callan had been his first – and only – adult relationship. At the time, he had been convinced that he would never need anything more, that Callan was the one and only person for him. And when that had fallen apart, he'd been devastated. Did he want to open himself up to the possibility of being hurt like that again?

"Why, because I'm one of your favorite places?"

"Well, of course."

He rolled his eyes. "A person can't be a place."

"They can be if that person is home."

Shane's nostrils flared, furious that he had the audacity to say something like that after the way they'd left things. "I don't think so, Cal. Maybe if we were strangers..."

"Why can't we be?" he asked in a hushed tone.

"You want a clean slate?"

It was something to consider. In their six months together, Shane had managed to keep all of his secrets, including his health. He had fallen hard, and fast, and he didn't want that to happen again. If they were even going to consider speaking to one another, it needed to be on *his* terms.

"Okay. If we're going to play that game, it'll be by *my* rules." When Callan didn't protest, he went on. "I'll text you a time and a place and we'll meet for the first time all over again."

Callan smiled. "I'm looking forward to it."

"Are you now?" Shane lifted the cell phone in his hand. "Things have changed since the last time we saw each other. *I've* changed. And you're going to be treated just like anyone else."

He furrowed his brow before nodding. "Okay...are you going to tell me what that means?"

"I guess you'll find out. Is your number still the same?"

"Yes. Do you remember it?"

"Of course I remember it, you idiot."

After checking to make sure there was no oncoming traffic, Shane walked through the parking lot, waving his hand in the air.

"Good luck!"

FALL 2009

"You're Shane, right?" came a voice from behind him.

He stopped and turned around, furrowing his brow when he saw that it was the boy who had been occupying his thoughts lately – Jake Talbot. "Yeah, that's me."

"I've been watching you."

"Oh." Not knowing how to take that, he lowered his gaze. "Sorry."

"Why are you apologizing?"

He shrugged. "This is usually the part where someone tells me I've done something wrong."

"*You're silly.*" *Jake smiled.* "*I like that. I mean, I like* you."

"*Oh!*" *This was turning out to be a very different conversation than what he'd expected. This seemed too good to be true.* "*Just to clarify-*"

"*I like, like you.*" *His smile spread across his cheeks.* "*And I was wondering if you'd like to go out sometime.*"

Eyes widening slightly, he took a quick look around to see if anyone had heard them. How could Jake say something like that out loud? How was he that comfortable?

"*Like, on a date?*" *Shane whispered.*

"*Well, it doesn't have to be, unless you want it to be.*" *His voice had softened. He could probably see the panic in Shane's features.* "*We could be friends, I'm cool with that.*"

His parents would say that he was going to Hell for this. To them, even thinking about another boy in a romantic manner would solidify his fate. Well, if Shane was damned anyway, why not actually experience the sin? "*I want it to be a date. I've never been on one before.*"

"*Really?*" *Jake raised his brow.* "*With a smile like yours?*"

Cheeks turning red, he cleared his throat uncomfortably. "*It's nothing special.*"

"*Hmm. I'll have to convince you otherwise.*" *There was a confidence about Jake that he admired. How could he be so sure of himself, so at ease with the world around him?*

"*What's your number so I can call you?*" *Jake asked.*

The color drained from his face. The very thought of the other boy calling either of his parent's numbers, and one of them answering, made Shane feel nauseous. "*Oh, um, it's probably best if you didn't. I mean, my parents are...*"

"*It's okay, I get it.*" *He nodded slowly.* "*How about lunch at Murphy's Diner, Saturday at two o'clock?*"

That, he could manage. Teenage boys met up with their

friends for lunch – his parents wouldn't suspect a thing. "I'll be there."

THIS WAS HIS INVENTION BUT IT WAS A NEW ONE, SO HE WAS curious as to how it would turn out. It was just a matter of time before one of them called it quits, thus losing the game. Shane was quite certain that he would outlast Callan – he always had, no matter what aspect of their relationship it had been.

He wished that they could have picked up where they'd left off, but he was a different person now. All he wanted was to fall into Callan's arms and melt away. The love was still there. It had never left.

That was something he was going to keep to himself; he couldn't lay all his cards on the table just yet. Maybe not ever. That would be giving Cal too much power and he was never going to do that again.

He walked to the park and up one of the trails with a stride in his step. It was a strange combination of emotions to be feeling – excitement, anxiousness, anger, and fear. All because of Callan. But this was not news to him and his damaged heart. He had known the moment he'd met the man, even at the tender age of eighteen, that Cal would be *the one*. Too bad it hadn't lasted. Though, even now, he would do anything for him.

When there was a fork in the trail, Shane sat on the bench between the two paths. There was a wooden railing meant to keep curious hikers from straying and falling down a declining hill.

He was taking solace in the few moments of silence before Callan's inevitable presence would interrupt him.

This time when he heard his voice, Shane closed his

eyes, wanting to pretend for just another moment that they were truly strangers, and that they could start over.

Then, taking a deep breath, he turned around, squinting from the sun. "I'm not moving. This is my spot."

"I wasn't going to ask you to move," he said with a smile. "On the contrary, I was hoping that you would let me take your picture."

"Oh." Raising an eyebrow, he glanced at the camera around Cal's neck. "You're a photographer, huh? I'm not very photogenic."

"That's nonsense." He waved his hand. "I'm a photographer slash journalist. Photography is my true passion but journalism is a close second. I can take you from behind..." Cal allowed the sentence to linger before clarifying. "Your picture, I mean. I can take it from the back so that your face doesn't show if you're self-conscious."

This seemed too familiar, too close to home – him posing in various places while his lover gushed over him and took dozens of pictures, capturing him in every light and at every angle. He was tempted to call off this whole game, afraid of where it might lead, but he couldn't bring himself to say goodbye. Not again. "What's in it for me?"

He laughed. "I can pay you for your trouble. I don't get paid much to begin with, but I can split my commission with you."

"Oh, I couldn't do that. Starving artist that you are." He paused. "Why don't you buy me dinner and we'll call it even?"

"Done. Though, if it's alright with you, I'd like to take a few different pictures."

"You're the artist." Shane shrugged. "Just as long as there are no expectations..."

"No, of course not. You're doing me a favor." He smiled in

a way that Shane yearned for on most days. "We can change the rules as needed."

Was that a hint? A sign that they could adapt to whatever Shane wanted or *needed* this to be? So far, this was working out well for him. That was the way he wanted it, since he had been the one who had been hurt last time.

"Fine." He extended his hand. "Name's Shane."

"It's nice to meet you." He shook it. "I'm Callan, but my friends call me Cal."

"Am I your friend?"

"I hope so."

A small smile crept along his cheeks. He pretended to admire the scenery while waiting for Cal to photograph him. "Well, go on. Take your shot."

Click.

"Got it."

"Just one?"

"For now."

Shane turned back around to face him. "So, where are we eating?"

"There's a new restaurant not far from here." He gestured for the younger man to follow him. They walked side by side down the path and out of the park. When they reached the parking lot, Cal turned to him.

"Would you like to take my car?"

"You expect me to get into a car with a stranger?" He smirked. "I'll follow you there."

With a chuckle, Cal shrugged. "Suit yourself."

Shane got into his own vehicle and then followed Callan's. This was where he could cheat a little at his own game. If he got lost, he could call or text, not that he would. He might simply drive away and leave the man wondering what had happened. It all depended on his mood.

When they pulled into the fancy restaurant from the other day, Shane rolled his eyes. He wanted to protest, but since they were pretending as if that day hadn't happened, he couldn't really do that.

Once inside, Callan took a seat, and so did Shane, directly across from him.

"Tell me," came the man's voice, smooth as silk, "Do you always agree to pose for strangers?"

"Only if they pay me," Shane answered with a smirk.

Callan paused, a small smile on his lips as his gaze wandered over the younger man. "So, you didn't think I was strange?"

Scratching the back of his neck nervously, he attempted to relax in his chair. Callan's attractiveness was intimidating, but he didn't want to mention that – it would only make him feel more awkward. There were things he wanted to say but couldn't for the sake of keeping up the charade. "Maybe a little. But I love art in every form, so I kind of understand the creative process...as much as I can without *being* an artist."

"It sounds like you have experience with the creative process then."

"A little."

When a glass of wine was placed in front of him, Shane was slightly caught off-guard because they hadn't bothered to ask for his ID, but he'd never been one to complain about alcohol. "I guess I've reached that magical time in my life where I don't look underage, huh? This is the first time I haven't been carded."

Another person brought food to their table. Luckily, it was Fettuccine Alfredo, something he liked, but it was a bit odd in his opinion. It made him uncomfortable that he hadn't been able to make the decision himself.

"You must be a regular here.They knew what to bring you."

"Yes," Callan said with a smile. "I've been here almost every day since they've opened. I bring a lot of clients here."

"Clients? I thought you were a journalist."

"I am, but that's more on the side." The tone of his voice lowered. "My father runs a law firm. Since I'm his only child, naturally, I have been expected to work there from the moment I was born."

Shane nodded slowly, having already known this, but not wanting to break character. "So, you don't like being a lawyer?"

"No." He scrunched his nose. "It sucks the soul out of you."

He wanted to say, *is that why you left me – because you had no soul?* And if he was still a lawyer, what made this time so different from the last?

"That's a shame," he mumbled. "I'd hate to be stuck in a job that made me miserable."

"Ah, finally, the subject turns to you." Callan smiled and gestured to him. "I'd like to know more about you, Shane. If you'll let me." He took a sip of his wine. "Describe yourself in six words."

"Six words? Only six?" Holding up his hand, he counted each word with his fingers for emphasis. "I'm a pain in the ass." He reached for his glass before taking a swig. "No, really. Just ask anyone who knows me."

Callan could only shake his head. "You know, I don't see that about you."

"Oh, just you wait." Shane held his gaze, almost daring him. Getting close to him would be no easy feat, especially not now.

"Alright, I won't argue with you," he responded in a

small voice. "I consider myself to be an agreeable person. I avoid confrontation if I can help it."

"If you don't argue with anyone, ever, then how can you ever have make-up sex?" He held back a laugh as the older man nearly choked on his wine. "Any other questions?"

"No," Cal answered cautiously. "Do you have any for me?"

Muddling it over in his mind, Shane enjoyed some of his food before speaking again. "Do you plan to quit the law firm at some point?"

Callan opened his mouth and closed it again. "I've been groomed to take over, but I would prefer not to. I guess I'm hoping to prove to myself that I can make enough off of journalism to survive. My father hasn't been kind about it." He paused again. "I've worked for what I have, I don't want anyone to think I've had it easy. I've sacrificed things that have mattered most to me in order to be where I am. Relationships," he clarified.

Running his tongue along his front teeth, Shane shook his head, muttering, "You don't know anything about sacrifice."

Silence fell between them. He took that time to finish his meal and sip his wine. Then, seeing the defeated look on Callan's face, he couldn't help but feel sympathy for him. It was his fault the man's face looked that way, after all. And if they were going to continue the game, he needed to watch his mouth.

It was getting later, and, having looked at the time, he realized that he was overdue for a dose of medication. He'd forgotten in all the excitement. "I should get going."

"Oh," Cal spoke in a hushed tone.

Shane couldn't hide that he was satisfied by the man's disappointment. He had to fix it though. As painful as it was, he was having fun too. "Maybe I can buy you dinner next time. Just not in a place like this."

"Oh!" Callan said in a much more cheerful voice. "Well, how does Friday sound? I mean, if you don't already have plans."

"Eh, I can move some things around." There was hardly ever a time when he was actually busy, but he wasn't going to tell him that. "Me leaving is more out of necessity. Believe me, I'd much rather stay here with you." That was too much. He hadn't meant to give Callan any indication that he still liked him. "My apartment is really, really boring. You're a slight improvement." There, had he fixed it?

Before he gave the man too much hope, Shane casually – and completely intentionally – brushed against Callan on his way out.

That night in his small apartment felt just as lonely as it had on the night Callan had left him. It was all coming back as fresh as the tears forming in his eyes.

And those weren't the only memories he was reliving lately.

This was a bad fucking idea. It was supposed to be fun, a segue to some sort of happy medium of what they had and whatever they might become.

He would have to adjust the rules as needed.

They hadn't even been around each other for two full days and he already wanted to throw himself at Callan, despite all evidence to the contrary.

Being so angry at someone, and wanting to jump their bones, and saying every mean thing he could think of, wasn't healthy.

No matter how much he wanted to, they couldn't pick up where they had left off. Shane wanted to pretend the past had never happened and simply move forward, but that wasn't realistic. Sooner or later, the past would come back to haunt him. And they would need to address it when it did.

If he couldn't count on Callan to be there for him when he'd been at what he considered to be his best, how could he trust Callan to be there when he was at his worst?

Winter 2009

It was after dark. He was supposed to be at his father's house, but he'd broken the rules. It was worth the risk.

"Shane, can I ask you something?"

"I think you just did," he teased.

There was a pause.

"Are you ashamed of me?"

Shane furrowed his brow. "What?"

"It's just..." Jake's voice trailed off as he lowered his gaze. "We've been going out for three months now and you won't let me kiss you or even hold your hand in public."

"It's not because I'm ashamed." How was this boy so unaware of how happy he made Shane? Maybe it was because he had nothing to compare it to. With everyone else, Shane was hiding, whether it was because of his father, his sexuality, or how completely inadequate he felt in all things — he could never truly be himself. Except with Jake. He'd done a poor job of expressing that.

"You're the best thing that's ever happened to me," he spoke with a soft smile. "I just don't want anything to ruin that."

While Jake's features lit up considerably, he didn't return the smile. "Does that mean I'm not going to meet your family?"

Shane chewed his bottom lip anxiously before shaking his head. "Believe me, you don't want to."

There was another pause. He had gotten pretty good at inter-

preting those. *This one said that Jake didn't necessarily believe him, but didn't want to say so.* "Are they really that bad?"

"You have no idea," he whispered.

Jake placed his hands on his hips, his eyes narrowed. "I don't want to be a secret. I want you to be proud to be with me."

"I am! How can I prove it to you?" Shane's gaze wandered over their surroundings in search of a solution to their problem. "Find a building we can climb – I'll shout it from the rooftops."

He rolled his eyes. "You're afraid of heights."

"Maybe so, but I'd still do it for you."

When Jake's cheeks flushed red, Shane's immediately followed suit.

Had he fixed it? Wanting to make their relationship public and being able to do so were two very different things. He just knew that if he didn't at least give Jake something to work with, this would end.

"Are you mad at me?" he asked in a small voice, taking Jake's hand in his.

"No," Jake responded, much to his relief. "I'm not mad."

2

Shane walked into a stone and gem shop called *Shiny Things* and saw his boss behind the counter. That was rare, but since he was the only employee, he hadn't left the owner much of a choice.

The middle-aged man clicked his tongue and shook his head. "You're late, kid."

He heaved a sigh and shooed the man from behind the counter so that he could take his place there. "When will you stop calling me that?"

"When you stop acting like one."

With a roll of his eyes, he leaned against the counter. "I overslept, Peter. And I'm sorry, but I can't promise that it won't happen again."

"Is everything okay?" Peter asked with a raise of his brow.

Shane shrugged, unwilling to give his boss a list of his problems. He never wanted to use his condition as an excuse. "I'm fine."

"It's okay if you're not." Peter walked over to one of the

shelves and shifted a few of the stones. "You don't have to be here every day if you're not feeling up to it."

"The day I can't do my job, I'll let you know. Will you lay off now?"

"Sure, as long as you don't make a habit of being late."

Since there was no one in the shop, he took the opportunity to sort out invoices that were sitting behind the counter. He thought the matter was settled but caught Peter staring at him.

"So...what's your excuse?"

Shane clicked his tongue. "I don't have one."

"Was it a girl?"

"No."

"Was it a boy?"

He pursed his lips before responding. "Yes and no."

With a smile, he took a step closer. "Come on, spill."

They had never spoken about their personal lives before, so this sudden interest made him suspicious. He had to remind himself that not everyone was out to get him. "When I was eighteen, I knew that I'd met the love of my life. He was everything I had hoped to find in a person. There was just one problem."

He cocked his head curiously. "He was married?"

"No," Shane mumbled with a scoff. "His family is...less than evolved. And he couldn't be in a relationship that his family wouldn't accept." He ran his tongue over his front teeth, the thought leaving a bad taste in his mouth. "So he left me."

"That's a shame." Peter dipped his chin and then raised his brow. "I assume there's more to this story."

"Why are you all up in my business today?" He shifted uncomfortably. "He's back in town and we sort of went on a date."

"And?"

"And I don't know if I can forgive him for leaving."

"That does pose a problem." He nodded slowly. "Were you happy to see him again?"

"I guess so. But I was kinda pissed too." Shane folded his arms. "If I hadn't bumped into him, I don't think I ever would have known that he was back. He wouldn't have reached out, he's too chickenshit."

"Hold the phone." Peter held up his hands. "You randomly bumped into, arguably, the love of your life?"

"Yeah. So?"

"That shit only happens in the movies. Unless it's fate."

Shane made a face. "You believe in fate?"

"Sure, why not?"

"Oh, god." He rolled his eyes. "Are you a hopeless romantic?"

"Romantic, not so much." Peter smirked. "Hopeless, absolutely."

He didn't know what had gotten into his boss today, but it was amusing, to say the least. It did make him wonder if he was going to suffer through this awkward bonding every day now. "Can we stop talking about my love life if I promise not to be late again?"

"That sounds fair." After shooting Shane a stern look, the older man disappeared behind a shelf. "The next time you're late, I'll be knocking down your door."

New Year's Eve 2009

People were lighting off fireworks. It seemed that everyone in the neighborhood was celebrating the holiday except for them. It was times like these when he wished that he didn't have to spend any holidays with his father, but fair was fair in the eyes of the court, and parents had to split holidays. He'd be having a much better time at home with his mother and brother.

The only saving grace of the evening was the puppy seated beside him on the couch. The young German Shepard's paws were draped over his lap as he flipped through TV channels.

He heard the shuffling of feet and looked over to the doorway of the kitchen where his father stood. The puppy lifted its head, both ears raised – one of them looking as though the tip had been cut off.

"Come here, Shane," the man said gruffly. "You're going to learn something today."

He knew that tone. It meant that his father was in a bad mood. "Can I put Teddy in my room first?"

"No, he's getting dragged into this because of you."

Fearing for the safety of the dog, he wanted to stand up, and, fearing for his own, he didn't want to move. "Into what?"

"I saw you in town...holding hands with that boy."

He was unable to hide panic-stricken features. Even if it hadn't been true, his father wouldn't have believed him. "Dad, we were joking around. We're just friends."

"You're a terrible liar. My own son, a fucking fairy." The adult who towered over him on a normal day seemed exponentially large in this moment, every step forward making Shane's heart race a bit faster. "That just breaks my heart, Shane. So now I'm going to break yours."

"Can I please put Teddy away?" he asked, his voice cracking.

"No."

Gently moving the puppy off his lap, Shane got to his feet, his hands shaking. As his gaze lowered, he noticed that his father was wearing his steel toe boots. The first thought that came to his mind was that he was going to kick Teddy to death. Shane had been on the receiving end of those boots. He was young, but he was stronger – Teddy was just a baby.

"*This is where the lesson comes in.*" *The man crossed his arms and dipped his chin, staring down his son. "It's you or the dog. Choose.*"

This was new. Usually when he was given a choice, it was between fist or boot, belt or paddle, Russian roulette or five finger fillet. He was always the one being hurt. He'd never been faced with the possibility of someone else being hurt because of him.

"*No,*" *he whispered desperately. "No, I'll do anything...please.*"

"*You have five seconds to decide, Shane.*" *The floor shook from the motion of his boots. "Five, four, three, two-*"

As soon as he was within reach, Shane's father grabbed the puppy by its neck. Shane rushed into action, using all his strength to pry his father's fingers from Teddy's throat and then shoving him away.

"*Stop it, leave him alone!*" *Swallowing hard, Shane glanced toward the dog to make sure he was alright. Teddy was whining with wide, alarmed eyes, and his ears pinned down. He must have been scared out of his mind. Shane knew the feeling. "Hurt me instead, I can take it.*"

"*You stupid piece of shit.*" *His father shook his head. "What kind of idiot chooses to save a dog's life over his own?*"

Idiot or not, Shane wasn't going to stand by and watch the innocent pup murdered before his eyes. He couldn't control much, but he could do something about this.

"*Teddy, come!*"

He secured the leash to his dog's collar in record time and exited through the front door — using the back one would have meant getting past his father. And he wasn't confident that he would be able to do that without Teddy getting caught in the crossfire.

Shane walked until his legs were sore, and then beyond that. Fireworks were being set off and the dog was becoming anxious. This was his plan, to leave Teddy alone and confused, so that he wouldn't be able to find his way home. It was better than what awaited them there.

They hadn't been together very long, but Teddy was smart. He was not only loyal to Shane but listened to him well. He was counting on that now. Veering off the sidewalk, he led the puppy to a wooded area and removed the leash and the collar. Hopefully, someone would assume he was a stray and take him in.

"Okay, Teddy. You have to stay here. You can't follow me, okay?"

The dog stared at him with a blank expression. A lump formed in his throat, tears blurring his vision.

"Stay," he repeated.

Turning his back on Teddy, he took a few steps forward and then quickly turned around to make sure that the dog was listening to his command, but he wasn't. "You can't come back with me! He's going to kill you, don't you understand?"

No, how could he? All the dog knew was that Shane was abandoning him. He would never know the reason behind it. As much as this pained him, he knew that he was saving Teddy's life. This wasn't the first time his father had threatened the pup and it wouldn't be the last. Even if Shane made sure that Teddy was at his mother's house full time, he was worried that his father would find a way to get to him.

Taking a deep breath, he threw his arms around Teddy. "I love you. I'm really sorry about all this."

He stood straight once more and wiped his tears on the sleeve of his shirt.

"Stay," he commanded for a third time.

Then he walked out of the wooded area and toward the side-walk. He looked over his shoulder every few minutes to be certain that Teddy wasn't following him. No sign of him, thank goodness.

It was dark by the time he returned to his father's house. Fire-works were still lighting up the town of Westbourne. Even with *all that noise, he was still startled by the hand on the back of his head when he walked in the door. The force knocked him to the floor and he pursed his lips, though he dared not move. Sometimes making eye contact worsened his father's mood.*

"If you ever put your hands on me again, I'll kill you, Shane."

CALLAN WAS WORRIED THAT SHANE WAS GOING TO CALL IT off. Everything was on his terms, and rightfully so, but it meant suspension in limbo. He was walking on eggshells, not knowing what Shane would do from one moment to the next.

They met at a modest restaurant this time because Shane was paying. This wasn't a place that Callan's family would have been caught dead in, and he couldn't have been happier about it as his date approached the table.

"Fancy meeting you here," he said with a grin.

"Haha, very funny." Shane sat across from him.

Callan could sense the obvious tension and his smile fell, though he quickly tried to recover with another smile. "I feel like we've talked a lot about me and not nearly enough about you. What is it that you do, Shane?"

"I work at a stone and gem shop. Sounds boring, I know. But it's usually quiet and relaxing."

"No, that sounds nice. I wish I could work in a place like that."

"You could do anything." Shane folded his arms. "I think your fear of losing your money and status keeps you at a job you hate."

Callan pursed his lips, the tension in the air finding its way to his jaw. "I have responsibilities. Obligations."

"Everyone does."

A waitress came by to take their orders, and while the

break in eye contact might have calmed any other person and made them adjust their attitude, it didn't have that effect on Shane.

"I just don't think you should complain about how miserable you are if you're not willing to do something about it."

Cal paused. "I'm trying."

"Are you?"

He swallowed hard, wondering if they were still playing the game. Until Shane said that they weren't, he was going to keep at it. "How can you be so judgmental when you don't know anything about me?"

"I know enough."

Cal heaved a sigh. "I suppose you've never made a mistake or felt like you had to please everyone. We don't all have the luxury of telling our parents to screw themselves." The twitch in Shane's face almost made him regret his words, though he deserved it as far as Cal was concerned. "My job makes me miserable but maybe I don't know who I am without it. Maybe I don't know how to reduce my life-style. Does that make me a bad person?"

"No." Shane took a sip of his water, letting the silence linger for a moment. "But making promises you can't keep doesn't make you a good one."

Cal shook his head. "So if people don't live up to your almighty standards, that makes them terrible? People make mistakes, Shane."

"And I'm one of yours, right?"

He furrowed his brow, staring into the stoic face of the younger man. It was so difficult to read him. Was he actually hurt or was he just trying to get under Callan's skin? Hurt, angry, whatever Shane was, it confused him.

Wanting to get this night back on track, he took a deep

breath and softened his tone. "If it's alright with you, I'd like to enjoy our dinner without prejudice. Can we do that?"

"You know, let's not kid ourselves here," he said abruptly. "This isn't going to work."

Callan's mouth fell open as he tried not to look as defeated as he felt. "Did I do something wrong?"

"No, this just isn't going to work for me." Shane got up from the booth, leaving a tip for the waitress on the table, and offering a small smile. "Sorry for wasting your time."

Cal was more concerned about the void in his life than he was about his wasted time. Ever since his departure, something had been missing. He'd thought that, in time, his love for Shane would fade, but it never had. And his fear of being happy in the past had now ruined any hope for their future.

JANUARY 2010

"What are we?"

The laughter of Jake's friends filled his ears. They were playing football and Shane was being a killjoy on the bench. Poor Jake probably felt obligated to sit with him.

"I don't know," he mumbled.

Rubbing his face with his hands, Jake let out an exasperated sigh. "I could have anyone, Shane. I could be dating someone who isn't ashamed to be seen with me."

"It's not that." *He hated that look of annoyance on the other boy's face. For a fourteen-year-old, he had shown Shane a lot of patience. And just like everyone else, he was getting fed up. Could Shane blame him though?* "Look, you don't understand, my family is-"

"Would you stop using your family as a crutch? They can't be that bad."

Why wouldn't anyone take him at his word? Why did people keep insisting that he was exaggerating? Why did they demand to know the specifics of his situation to decide whether or not he was telling the truth? Maybe he was expecting too much. He belonged in a cave somewhere, that way he wouldn't have to explain anything to anyone, he wouldn't be bothered, and they wouldn't get annoyed with him.

Gritting his teeth, he stood from the bench and lowered his voice. "I'm trying to protect you."

Jake threw his hands in the air. "From what?"

"I can't tell you!" A few of Jake's friends looked in their direction. His cheeks flushed red from embarrassment. "I really like you, Jake. It's just..." No. It was too much for Jake to handle. He was living it and didn't know how he kept going day to day. How could he put that on another person?

"We're the same age, Shane. Stop acting like I'm not old enough to understand whatever you're hiding from me. I don't want to keep playing these games with you." Shane opened his mouth to speak but Jake raised his hand to silence him before walking away. "Figure out what you want and then come find me."

WITH A GROAN, HE TILTED HIS HEAD, CRACKING HIS NECK. HE couldn't help fidgeting. Hopefully, this would cheer him up, because he'd been in a bad mood for years and Callan was making it worse. Though, if he was being honest with himself, he had to admit that being away from Cal was contributing to said bad mood.

He just couldn't let the man walk back into his life, not now that his view of love and life were so different. Less hopeful. Much, much less. A lot had changed in the years since Cal had been away, and not for the better.

A smile was instantly brought to his face when he heard a knock on the door, and a family of four arrived that consisted of his brother, sister-in-law, and niece and nephew.

"Uncle Shane!" the boy yelled as he ran toward him.

Shane knelt on the floor and opened his arms. "Harper and Hayden!" The children wrapped their small limbs around him. "Oh, you guys give the best hugs."

"Better than daddy?" Harper asked.

"Definitely better than daddy," he said with a chuckle.

"Excuse me, I think I'm a fabulous hugger," his brother spoke confidently.

Shane got to his feet before giving his brother a hug. "Good to see you, Ethan." When he let go, he smiled politely at his sister-in-law. "Hey, Nora."

"Hi, Shane," she said with a nod.

He closed the door behind them and ushered everyone into his humble apartment. "I'm so happy you guys are here."

Ethan ruffled Shane's hair. "They were thrilled when we told them that we were moving closer to you and mom. It's for purely selfish reasons, of course. Nora was transferred to this department, and then that bar just happened to be for sale in town. And here we are!"

His older brother had always worked in bars or restaurants, taking every position to learn the ins and outs of the business. Having a place of his own had always been a dream of his, and Shane was glad that it just happened to be so close.

"What a stroke of luck, huh?" He ruffled Ethan's hair in return.

"Now you don't have to be by yourself anymore!" Harper exclaimed.

"That's right!" He laughed awkwardly and scratched his ear. "I'm free to babysit any time."

"Are you sure?" Nora asked. "We don't want you to put yourself under any unnecessary stress."

"These guys don't cause stress, they relieve it." The expression on her face showed hesitance in believing his answer. He couldn't blame her because they hadn't spent much time together in-person. They had never liked each other, but he adored the kids. "I don't know about anyone else, but I'm starving."

Ethan raised his brow, looking toward the kitchen. "Did you make dinner?"

"No, but I ordered it." He rubbed his hands together, grinning at his niece and nephew. "Same difference, right?"

While the twins helped themselves to the TV, Nora inched toward the door. "Well, I'm going to leave you to it. I'll see you guys at home."

"See you later, mom!"

Harper and Hayden waved to their mother as she exited the apartment and then went back to the distraction of technology.

Grabbing a few paper plates, Shane kept his voice low. "Nora doesn't like me, huh?"

"You don't like her either," Ethan mumbled.

He shrugged. "Sure I do."

"Well, you don't show it."

Shane set the paper plates on his round dining table. "I'm like that with everyone."

"That bothers her, you know." He paused. "The way you talk to people."

"And how would she know how I talk to people?"

"She sees your social media. She hears you over the phone sometimes." Ethan's mouth fell open momentarily while trying to come up with more examples. "And I, you know, sometimes tell her about our conversations."

Shane chuckled and shook his head. This wasn't news; everyone walked on eggshells around him. In his opinion, that was there problem, not his. "I don't care what she thinks of me, just like I'm sure she doesn't care what I think of her."

"Shouldn't you care? She's my wife, the mother of your niece and nephew."

He furrowed his brow. "Of course I care. But I'm not going to change. She wouldn't and neither would you."

Ethan gave him a stern look. "We don't have anything that we need to change."

He raised his hands defensively. "Oh, sorry, I didn't know I was dealing with models of perfection."

"You know what I mean, Shane." He rolled his eyes. "You're difficult to deal with sometimes. You're even doing it right now. Shane the Pain."

There was a knock on the door, this time signaling the arrival of food, so he grabbed his wallet from the counter. "Okay, I'll try to remember to sugarcoat my personality around you."

"Yeah, an attitude adjustment would do you good."

FEBRUARY 1ST 2010

"Sweetie, the phone's for you." Shane walked over to his mother and took the phone from her hand. There was concern in her gaze which meant that something had happened, something that she thought would upset him. Had they found Teddy? Had his father made good on his threat?

Chewing his bottom lip nervously, he pressed the phone to his ear. "H-hello?"

"Shane, this is very important, I need you to listen to me." To his surprise, it was Jake's mother. She sounded frantic.

"Of course, Missus Talbot. What is it?"

"When was the last time you saw Jake?"

"I...well, I haven't seen him since last week." He paused, dreading to ask, but knowing he had to. "Is everything okay, Missus Talbot?"

"No," she answered breathlessly. "He didn't come home last night. If you see him or hear anything, will you call me? I know how close you two are. It isn't like him to leave without telling you, or us, or anyone...you know that, don't you?"

He swallowed hard, tears welling up in his eyes. "Yes, Missus Talbot. He's a happy kid. He wouldn't just leave without a word."

The poor woman choked back a sob. "Thank you. I guess I just needed to hear that. The police think he's a runaway, so they're not really looking for him..."

"I'll help you look for him. My mom will bring me over."

"Thanks, kiddo. That means a lot to me."

When she hung up, he handed the phone back to his mother. "I can ask Ethan to drive me if you don't want to," he said quietly.

"Don't be silly, honey." She pulled him into a tight embrace. "Your friend is missing. Of course I'm going with you."

His friend. Jake's family knew about him, but Shane couldn't return the favor. In fact, if he told his mother what Jake meant to him, she would not only refuse to go looking for him, but she would forbid Shane from trying to do so as well. All he could do was pray to God – the same God his mother said would condemn him – that Jake would be found safe.

IT WAS A SLOW DAY AT THE SHOP. MOST OF THE TIME, SHANE was there to open and close. He practically ran the place. Even though his boss had made it clear that he didn't need the money from the shop, Shane certainly did, and he was the only employee other than Peter.

He didn't mind because he enjoyed it there; it was peaceful and stress-free – just what the doctor ordered, literally.

He had permission to close up early if no one had come in for a solid two hours. It was around that time. Refreshing social media to pass the last few minutes, he heard the bell on the door signaling that someone had come in. Normally, he would have been a little annoyed – disappointed that he couldn't go home early. But the person perusing the shop took his breath away, as the man had done on many occasions before.

Shane's gaze followed Callan moving from shelf to shelf, obviously pretending that he had no idea it was Shane behind the counter. When their gazes met, he cleared his throat uncomfortably. "Anything I can help you find, sir?"

"Well, that depends." He smiled awkwardly as he approached the counter. "Are you in the business of forgiveness?"

"No," he said without hesitation. When he gave it more thought, he knew that wasn't true. Being a shit was a knee-jerk reaction, but that automatic response didn't always speak to what he truly wanted. "I could be...persuaded. Maybe."

A look of relief washed over Cal's face and he nodded. "Do you, um, have a favorite stone?" He gestured around the shop.

Casually pushing his phone to the side, Shane's gaze wandered over the many shelves, as if he needed to give that some thought, but he didn't. He'd spent enough time there to know what crystals he preferred. It wasn't difficult to find something beautiful about each stone; they were all different and had unique qualities. Just like people. He'd never seen a rock that he thought was ugly. In fact, he adopted those for himself when no one else wanted them.

"Amethyst is really popular. So is Rose Quartz. People think they'll help in the love department. Personally, I prefer Emerald. My absolute favorite is Septarian." He gestured for Cal to follow him to another shelf where there sat a large Septarian egg. "How could I not love something that looks like it was forged by a dragon?"

God, this man smelled good. He stepped away to give Cal a better look at the stones, but, really, it was because he needed the space. He'd never struggled to maintain a professional manner before and he wasn't about to break that streak now. "It all depends on what you're looking for, honestly. Each crystal has a different purpose."

Cal smiled, his gaze moving back and forth between Shane and the stones. "So, if Rose Quartz and Amethyst don't help in the love department, what does?"

He opened his mouth and closed it again, knowing what his boss would want him to say, but he just couldn't help himself. "I'm supposed to sell you whatever I can in whatever *way* I can. If you think a stone will help you find love, I'm supposed to fluff you up with a bunch of bullshit. Thing is, I'm allergic to bullshit." It was a really good thing that there were no cameras there and that they weren't being recorded, otherwise he could be fired not only for swearing, but for what he was about to say. "If people's love lives are so bad that they're looking to a rock for help, they're probably a lost cause."

Callan laughed. "Don't look to rocks for help with your love life. Got it."

Shane shrugged, walking back toward the counter. "Stones are great for soothing things, attracting things, keeping things away, but they can't help you find love or keep it. They don't have that kind of power, only people do. Collecting rocks for that purpose is a convenient way for people to relinquish responsibility in the matter. It makes them feel better to believe that it's not their fault at all and chalk it up to bad luck. Not that I'm an expert on life. Or love."

He looked him over and shrugged. "You look pretty well-adjusted to me."

"Depends on who you ask. I'm an acquired taste, not for everyone. But with me, what you see is what you get. I don't hide who I am, what I think, what I feel. So at least everyone knows what they're getting into with me."

Silence lingered as they shared a long gaze. Shane had always been mesmerized by his blue eyes and had too much pride to look away because, to him, that would be like admitting defeat.

"Why did you come here?" Shane asked softly.

"Whatever I did to upset you the last time we met, I want to make it up to you."

Had he been too harsh? Had he been unfair? Maybe he hadn't given the man a fair chance. Despite everything that had happened between them, Shane missed Callan terribly. Was it normal to ache for someone who had broken your heart?

The ball was in his court. Cal had made that perfectly clear.

"The park. Near the trails. Tomorrow."

Something about those blue eyes rendered him incapable of speaking complete sentences. Callan didn't seem to mind as he smirked triumphantly, nodded, and then left the shop.

3

He couldn't say that his personal life had never affected his work before, but since the return of Cal, he found himself daydreaming a lot more.

The shop was slow today so the slight romantic in him had plenty of time to think about their future.

Peter came out of the back room with a glass in hand. Shane could only assume what was inside it. His boss had never been unprofessional, and he owned the place, so Shane wasn't going to protest.

He tried to look busy going through invoices and intakes, but Peter's gaze was glued to him. It was unnerving and he couldn't help but inquire.

"What?"

"Got any plans this weekend?"

"No."

"You do now."

He grimaced as though the thought was painful. "What?"

"I'm going to New York and you're tagging along."

"Aww, are you scared to go alone?" Shane couldn't help but smirk.

"You look like you haven't had fun in years." Peter gestured toward him with the drink in his hand. "Trust me, I'm doing you a favor."

This was unusual. They never spent time together outside of work. He had nothing against the older man, in fact, he liked him more than most people, but their relationship had never been anything but professional. What had changed? "And what have I done to deserve such generosity?"

"I work you to the bone." He walked up to the counter and emptied the contents of the glass into his mouth. "Consider it a bonus."

Shane wiggled his lips back and forth. Something was off here; he just couldn't place it. "Who's going to watch the store?"

"I'll close it for the weekend." Peter smirked. "Don't worry, I can afford it."

That had never been his worry. When it came to vibes, Shane had learned to trust his. If he'd ever thought that Pete was a bad guy in any way, he wouldn't be working for him. But something about this seemed strange. Had he found out about Shane's heart? If so, that was a serious invasion of privacy. "What is this about?"

"Jesus, relax, will you? I just want a weekend away. And, to be honest, I don't have anyone else to go with."

While he could certainly believe that, he also believed that there was more to the story. "You don't have any...friends? Or a girlfriend?"

"Me, friends?" He laughed and shook his head. "You know so little about me, kid."

Shane's tongue ran along his front teeth. He had to

admit that he'd always been curious about his boss, and now it seemed that his boss was curious about *him*. "I insist on paying for my portion of the trip."

"I invited you, I intend to pay."

He shook his head. "I want to pay my own way."

"Suit yourself."

Swallowing hard, he folded his arms to hide how uncomfortable he was by the idea, even though he'd just agreed to it. He didn't know Peter well enough to trust him. But there were certain things he was willing to take a chance on. "Okay, old man. I'll go. Only because there are some restaurants I'm dying to try."

"There will be no dying of any kind." He set his glass down on the counter. "I'm sure your parents would kill me."

He licked his lips. "Only one."

"You're in charge of the restaurants." Peter walked past the counter and continued to the back room. "I'll be in charge of attractions."

With a roll of his eyes, he grabbed the glass and tucked it behind the counter, out of view from potential customers.

Only God knew why he put himself in these situations. Why did he feel like he was going to end up babysitting a grown man?

When he'd closed up shop for the day, Shane returned home only to prepare for another outing.

After filling his backpack with the essentials – water, his medication, snacks, his fully charged cell-phone, and a flashlight, Shane ventured outside to hit one of his favorite trails. It had become his favorite because in all the times he'd walked through it, there hadn't been another soul. That was the way he liked it because it was supposed to be his time for peace and quiet. Sharing his favorite spot with Cal was going to be a challenge, but one that he was up for.

Two miles into the trail, he stopped when seeing a man with a camera. Even from behind, the man looked like a work of art.

Unexpectedly, another man approached Callan and mumbled something. Cal laughed, clapped the man on the back, and said something in response. Then the man continued on his way, oblivious to Shane's presence.

He thought about turning around right then and there, throwing in the towel on this whole thing. But Cal turned and flashed him a smile. And that was the end of that thought.

Shane pursed his lips, not knowing what to say. How exactly should he handle this situation? He was disappointed, though he had no right to be – he had known that Cal was well sought after. Always had been. As much as he flat out wanted to ask who that other man was, it was not his place, and if he didn't want people prying into *his* life, he couldn't very well pry into theirs.

"This is my favorite trail because it's usually empty. Seeing the, uh...two of you here has thrown me off a bit. I, uh-" He jerked his thumb in the direction behind him. "I should head back."

Cal furrowed his brow. "But you just got here. That was my friend. He's very, very straight, if that's what you're worried about."

"I'm not worried about anything," he snapped. "Don't flatter yourself."

Cal heaved a sigh and rubbed the back of his neck. "Would it be okay if I walked with you?"

How could Shane say no when he'd asked permission? He was a sucker for people abiding by his rules. It meant that they had listened, that they gave a shit. "Sure."

It seemed like much longer than a two mile walk back to

the entrance. His pride wouldn't allow him to carry on with their day as planned. What little confidence he'd had was shaken by seeing that other man, even though he believed Callan.

"You were quick to tell me how straight your friend was," Shane said. "Does that mean you've assumed I'm not?"

"Well, *I'm* not. So, by the way we've spoken, I guess I did make an assumption and I shouldn't have."

"No sweat." Shane shrugged. "I'm bisexual and I'm very comfortable with the idea. My mom, however, is not. She struggles between staying true to her religion and staying true to her son."

"I'm sorry. I know how parents can be. I was in denial for a while, but I've come to the determination that I'm also bisexual, and I lean toward men. But I'm not comfortable with it at all and neither are my parents."

As far as he was concerned, Callan's parents were the reason their relationship had ended in the first place. "Sorry to hear that."

The silence that followed didn't bother him because he was used to it, but it seemed to bother Cal, who spoke up.

"It's going to be a long walk back if you don't want to talk to me."

Shane opened his mouth to speak and then closed it, needing another moment to gather his thoughts. "It's not that I don't want to talk to you, but it's not...*I'm* not..." Clearly, he needed more time to consider his response.

The only people he held back for were his niece and nephew; everyone else got the same treatment. But there were moments in time, just like this one, where he tried to explain his actions or allude to the reasons behind his behavior. And, as always, he kept it vague, feeling unsafe, and stopped before he went too deep.

"You seem good. And I'm *not* good." Clearing his throat, he squinted with the sun in his eyes. "But we could be friends if you don't mind hanging around a rude, sarcastic asshole."

He stopped and gently placed his hand on the younger man's arm. "I don't know why you would say you're not good and that *I* am. I think you have that twisted." His touch lingered just long enough to make it awkward before they continued on. "I don't mind being around you. In fact, it's refreshing. The exercise might kill me if this becomes a regular thing though."

"I need to exercise but take it easy. Doctor's orders. That's what they tell me, *just relax, don't stress out*." Shoving his hands into his pockets to hide his fidgeting fingers, he trudged down the trail, gaze staring straight ahead. "I hate it when they tell me that. It's not like people can help how they feel."

"Do you have trouble relaxing?"

"You could say that. And yourself?"

"Oh, yeah. That would be an understatement. My friends frequently accuse me of having a stick up my ass."

"That's funny," he said with a smirk. "Considering our conversation earlier, I wouldn't think you'd mind having something up your ass."

Callan struggled getting words out of his mouth as his cheeks turned red. "Not sticks. Never sticks. Do you have any idea how rough they are?"

"Ah, so you don't like it rough?" Shane smirked again seeing the rest of Cal's face join the color of his cheeks. "That's good to know. For future reference."

"Can we talk about something else?"

"Sure. How's work?"

"Remember, me, *stick*? Work does that."

"Sounds like you have the wrong job."

"Well, we can't all afford to sell rocks. No matter how much we'd like to. You should see my bills."

"I guess that's why I sell rocks. I live a very simple life." He shrugged. "Materiel things mean nothing to me."

"Consider yourself lucky." Cal paused and pursed his lips. "You seem happy with who you are. I am anything but."

He raised his brow. "You don't like yourself?"

"No. Couldn't you tell?"

"You seem so...confident." Shane's gaze wandered over him. "I guess I'm at peace with who I am because I'm unwilling to change. But I never said I *liked* who I am."

"Well, I do." Cal looked at him. "Very much."

They came to the entrance sign which meant that it was time to part ways. And while Shane always missed him, this time was different than the previous ones. His chest felt heavy. He didn't want to leave, but he couldn't bring himself to say those words.

"Well..." There was a long pause before he continued. "See you next time, Cal."

"There *will* be a next time, right?"

"There has to be," he answered softly. "I don't think I could stand it if there wasn't."

FOLLOWING THE DIRECTIONS THAT PETER HAD GIVEN HIM, Shane found himself on a private runway. It took him a moment to realize that he and his boss would be the only people on the plane, other than the pilot.

"What the fuck?"

Peter slapped him on the back and then motioned for him to follow up the stairs and into the aircraft. "I have a private jet. Did I forget to mention that?"

"Uh...yeah." With a shake of his head, Shane stepped onto the jet. It looked nicer than his apartment. And most houses he'd seen. "I didn't know the shop was doing *that* well."

"It isn't. This is old money, kid. My family's swimming in it."

"You learn something new every day." He sat down across from Peter, furrowing his brow, his mouth open in awe. "I don't feel like I know you at all."

"Well, that's the point of this trip." Peter chuckled and offered him a drink. "To get to know each other."

"You do know that you're contributing to pollution, right?" He took the drink even though he couldn't have it.

"Yeah, yeah."

Shane shifted in his seat because he was supposed to get the okay from his doctor before traveling, and he hadn't done that. Now he was nervous, not because something might happen, but because Peter had no idea about his condition. He didn't like showing any kind of vulnerability in front of people in general, and especially not people he didn't know well.

"Don't tell me you're an anxious flier," Peter said with a laugh.

"No, I'm just-" He pursed his lips. It would have been so easy to tell him, and yet, he couldn't bring himself to do so. "Still uncomfortable with this whole thing, I guess."

"Relax, kid. This is supposed to be fun."

"Right." He swallowed hard before handing the drink back to Peter. "I didn't really want that, I was just being polite."

"Well, I appreciate your honesty. More for me."

After Peter downed two more drinks, the plane took off.

Shane waited for the pilot to give them permission to move before he helped himself to the couch.

"Will you be offended if I catch up on sleep?" he asked as he closed his eyes.

"Nah," Peter responded. "I've got plenty to keep me busy for a while. Sleep away."

Hours later, Shane woke with a gasp. It took several long breaths before he remembered where he was, and that he was safe.

"Christ, kid. Was the boogie man after you?"

Wiping his hand over his pale face, he sat up. "Something like that."

Peter lifted his chin. "Who's Jake?"

He swallowed hard. "What?"

"You mumbled that name."

"Um...nothing." Closing his eyes, he shook his head. "I mean, no one."

"Alright." Setting a magazine onto the empty seat next to him, Peter leaned forward toward the couch. "Are you sure you're feeling okay?"

He lifted his head. "Yeah, I haven't been getting a lot of sleep lately."

"Neither have I." He motioned to the seat opposite him. "You should buckle up, we're about to land."

Shane was quick to move back into the seat. He took solace in the distraction of the window.

"Do you have nightmares?"

"Yeah, kid." He tapped his temple. "I've got boogiemen too."

"Do you ever turn the tables on them?"

"Sometimes." Peter shrugged. "But more often than not, they win. Just like in real life."

"Yeah," he said with a scoff. "You're preaching to the choir."

There was relief when the plane landed. Shane felt like he could breathe again. They got into a cab and he checked his phone, not at all surprised that he'd missed a call from his mother.

"I'm going to meet up with some friends in the city," Peter said, also checking his phone. "You're welcome to join."

Shane raised an eyebrow. "I thought you didn't have any friends."

"I do in New York." He turned to look at him. "Do you have friends?"

"Not in New York." Shane smirked. "Are you concerned about my social life?"

"Let's just say I've noticed how much you work. And I don't want to be your excuse for missing out on life."

"Believe me, you're the least of my problems."

When they reached the hotel, Peter mumbled the accommodations to the receptionist. Shane wasn't paying much attention; he only knew to take the key and head to the room.

It hadn't necessarily been an unbearably long trip, but when he wasn't feeling well, and he was heading into something he really didn't want to do, that made it seem like forever.

Hearing the clicking of the closed door behind him, he breathed a sigh of relief and rolled his suitcase over to the closet area.

He turned on some lights, and then furrowed his brow, confused as to why there seemed to be so much space. This was certainly more than he was used to, and a far cry from his shitty apartment. This place was too good for him. He felt like sitting in the chair, or on the bed, or even using the bathroom would ruin the place just because he'd touched it.

"What the *fuck*," he muttered as he left his duffle bag on the floor. How he wished that Peter could have booked a room at a motel. Or a hostel. Anything but this. He didn't feel deserving of it.

With a groan, he threw himself onto the bed and closed his eyes. His head was throbbing and it would have been so easy to fall asleep, considering this was the most comfortable mattress he'd ever laid on.

Then he heard the click again, only this time, it came from the side wall. When a door opened, he realized that his room was adjoining to the room beside it. And Peter was standing in the doorway.

His jaw clenched and he was tempted to give the older man a piece of his mind. Something about choices and decisions, but Peter wouldn't understand any of that. And, after all, he was lucky that Peter had been nice enough to book him a room in the first place.

For his own peace of mind, he would have preferred to know about the rooms ahead of time. Someone having access to him at any and all times felt like a serious intrusion. This reminded him of things he'd rather forget – of being watched, of things coming with strings attached. But Peter meant no harm. He knew that.

Instead of lashing out, he smirked and put his hands behind his aching head. "Wow, I didn't know this room came with a personal butler."

"You wish." Peter stepped in his room, arms folded. "I'm sure your mother would kill me if anything happened to you. And since I invited you here, I thought it'd be a good idea to remain...close."

"What are you, my fucking babysitter?" Shane rolled his eyes. "What do you know about my mom anyway?"

"Uh...I know that she'd kill me if anything happened to you."

"How do you know that?"

"Because I'm a parent."

Shane pursed his lips, unsure whether or not he was surprised by that response. "And?"

"And I feel responsible for you. But if it really bothers you, I'll change rooms."

"It's fine," he grumbled as he sat up. "Just ask me next time."

"You got it, kid."

"And stop calling me kid, old man."

"That, I can't promise." Peter pulled the wallet from his pocket and handed Shane a credit card. "I have a few. I'm giving you this one for the weekend as long as you agree to try to have fun."

For a moment, he stared at it, unsure if it was a real offer or not. Now, this, he could accept. Options. Choices. The freedom to do whatever he wanted. How could he turn that down?

"Well, thanks."

"You're welcome. Just don't do anything I wouldn't do."

"But if we don't know each other very well yet, how am I supposed to know what you would and wouldn't do?" he asked with a sly smile.

Peter gave him a look. "Drugs. I'm talking about drugs."

"Don't worry, I'm not into that shit. Besides, I don't know if dealers accept credit cards." He flashed a grin before tucking the card into his bag of essentials.

As soon as Peter left to dinner, Shane took his daily dose

of medication – one of several – and then headed out for the evening, ready for a night of fun and forgetting his troubles.

This was every young person's wish – an unlimited budget. And what did young people typically do? Drink and do drugs. Both things that were off-limits for someone in his condition. There were times when he broke those rules, but he never went overboard. If there was one thing he was good at, it was self-control. At least, he liked to think so.

Troublemaker Shane didn't need drugs or alcohol to have a good time. With Peter's magical card, he took a few liberties and didn't feel guilty about it. He went shopping, ate the most expensive food he could find, dropped the new additions to his home collection at the hotel, and then went to a club. What else was there to do at night than dance in a room full of loud, sweaty people?

Night had become early morning and he needed sleep. Before retiring to his hotel, he used the restroom, and on his way out, someone pushed the door open forcefully. The door hitting his face made his eyes water. It shouldn't have been a big deal; the guy hadn't done it on purpose. The good thing was that it didn't really hurt after the initial sting, and after checking in the mirror, he knew his nose wasn't broken. And then he felt it, not just a trickle or slow drip, but a rush of blood.

As he pulled off his jacket, bunched it into his hands and pressed it to his nostrils, the horrified stranger apologized profusely.

"Don't worry, it's not you, it's me." He pushed past the stranger and the few people waiting outside the men's room, trying to think of a plan. His doctor had told him to go straight to the emergency room in an event like this, but what could they do for him? Prescribe more medication? The ones he was on could only do so much, though quitting them would shorten his life. And adding to them wouldn't change anything. What a mess.

After squeezing through the hoard of young people who didn't have a care in the world, he stood outside the building and contemplated whether or not to call Peter.

He didn't want to kill the old man's buzz – surely, he had one if he was out with friends. Or maybe he really was old and had been in bed for hours. Either way, Shane didn't feel right about disturbing him.

Taking a deep breath of fresh air, the world around him was going in and out of focus. He could get a taxi but was worried that he, should he become lightheaded, would be unable to give an address or pay the driver. Maybe texting Peter was an option. Something like, '*my nose won't stop bleeding, can you come and get me?*'

Jesus, no. That sounded childish. Why would one adult ask another adult to pick him up when they were still, in his mind, strangers?

A taxi it was. He managed to successfully give the driver the name of his hotel, and was dropped off in one piece. Being alone in the room made him feel slightly better.

Blood was dripping down his nostrils. Growling in frustration, he grabbed one of the hand towels. The bathroom was starting to look like a crime scene. He was past the point of concern – anyone in their right mind would have gone to the hospital.

But if he was admitted, he would be compelled to tell either his mother or his brother, who would then be compelled to tell either his mother or his brother. And when his mother knew, she would feel obligated to tell his father, because in some ways, she still considered them to be married. As far as Shane knew, she hadn't dated since the divorce. Her church was skilled in the art of shaming.

Even though he was well over the age of eighteen, and his father was nowhere near being on his list of emergency contacts, his mother still thought the man deserved to know everything about Shane's health. What parent wouldn't be interested in that information? He knew that his father couldn't have cared less, but he probably put on a show for Shane's mother.

The dilemma was to stay in the bathroom or to go to bed and risk messing up the sheets. If the unsuspecting maid became concerned about the suspicious state of the room, she might call the police, and he hated cops. Never found one he could trust. Once he explained his condition, it wouldn't matter whether or not they believed him – the blood was his and any test would prove that. But the thought of being put in another uncomfortable situation made the blood drip a little faster from his nose.

Finally, he decided on staying in the bathroom. He even managed to fall asleep. For how long, he didn't know, but something woke him up. A knock. He could only guess who it was.

The towel had fallen from his face and there was blood on his shirt, but it didn't appear to be new. Hopefully, the bleeding had stopped. But he felt the effects from the loss of it as soon as he stood up.

Shane had to steady himself on the sink. He washed the blood from his face, left the towel on the floor, and opened the door. Gripping the handle gave him somewhat stable support.

"Oh," he said, furrowing his brow. "Are you just getting in?"

"Yes," Peter said hesitantly, looking him up and down. "And by the state of you, it's a good thing I did."

The older man disappeared just for a moment and came back with a bucket of ice. "Want to tell me what happened?"

Taking the bucket of ice, he gestured for Peter to follow him. He went straight into the bathroom, took a clean hand towel, filled it with ice, and then pressed it to his nose. The flow might have stopped but it was better safe than sorry. "I'm on, um...I have..."

He was waving his hand, trying to think of the words, but his brain and his mouth weren't connecting. Whatever he tried to say wouldn't make much sense, and he didn't want to sound like an idiot, so he waited until he was able to fully form the words before speaking them.

"I'm on blood thinners," he explained. "I was leaving a club and this guy kinda swung the door into my face. It was an accident."

"You're on blood thinners?" Peter closed the door and helped the younger man to the table across the room. "How long have you been bleeding?"

"I don't know. I fell asleep. An hour, maybe?"

"Do you have a goddamn death wish?"

"No," he mumbled.

Peter paused. "I want you to be honest with me, Shane. Are you on drugs?"

"Do you really think I'm a coke-head?" He shook his head with a laugh. "Come on, man."

"Well, how am I supposed to trust you? Have you looked in a mirror?"

"So, bleeding automatically makes me a liar?"

"No, but considering how unconcerned you are with the situation, I have to wonder if it was self-inflicted."

"Well, it wasn't. I just fucking hate hospitals."

"I can't blame you, but I don't think you realize how serious this can be."

"Can we talk about something else?"

Peter eyed him warily. "Fine. You're an adult, I can't force you. But at least order some room service, alright?"

He couldn't deny that he was a bit hungry, and if he wasn't going to replace the blood he'd lost, the least he could do was fuel his body with something else. "Okay."

"Use the card, kid. Order whatever your black heart desires."

Shane couldn't help but smile even though it probably wasn't supposed to be funny. He was able to gather his senses and ordered whatever sounded good, which was, admittedly, quite a bit.

"Alright, while we wait, let's get to this getting-to-know-each-other business."

Shane shrugged. "Okay. What do you want to know?"

"For starters, what do you like to do in your spare time?"

Heaving a sigh, he fell back onto the bed and stared up at the ceiling. This was more conversation than he'd had all week. Were they trying to go for a record? Part of him felt like it was a trick. No one could be that interested in talking to him, not for this long.

"Are you asking because you're bored or because you feel obligated to make conversation?" Shane paused to rethink his response. If someone was genuinely interested in him, he should at least try to interact. "Normal things, I guess. I like being outdoors, listening to music, writing. What do you do besides pretend you're not loaded?"

Peter chuckled and shook his head. "I like drinking, dancing, traveling, trying new things. And I don't tell anyone I'm loaded because then they'll make more assumptions than they already do."

"And why would people make assumptions about you?"

He narrowed his gaze as if trying to decide whether or not he believed Shane. "You really don't know, do you?"

Shane shrugged. "If you mean I really don't know what you're talking about, that would be correct."

He was practically seeing stars but would never admit that he was close to passing out. A hospital was out of the question. No matter how much he may have needed one, or even wanted one at this point, fear made his thought process irrational. Nothing was worse than his father knowing where he was or what he'd been doing.

The food arrived and Shane was more than happy to let Peter retrieve it and bring it to the table. There were steaks, potatoes, green beans, bread, and chocolate milkshakes. None of that would go well together, however, his deprived body didn't care.

"You don't have to stay," he said in between bites. "I'll be fine."

"Do you want me to leave?"

"I don't want you to stay and I don't want you to leave. Being weak in front of people means I'm open to an attack. Now, I know you're not going to jump across the table and punch my lights out – at least, I hope not," he tapped his temple for emphasis, "but the PTSD doesn't."

Maybe it was the loss of blood, the exhaustion threatening to take over, or the unsteadiness of his breathing that made him aware of every symptom. Maybe it was knowing that if he didn't say anything, Peter would leave and they might never have this opportunity again. The need for sleep rendered his filter useless.

Peter stared at him for what seemed like hours, saying nothing, not touching the food on his plate. He looked as though he was contemplating his next words very carefully.

"Is there something you'd like to share with me, Shane?"

No. It wasn't safe. He hadn't meant to talk about his past, he'd only been trying to explain himself. Though, in order to do that, he did have to mention things he normally wouldn't.

"I was bullied a lot in school for being weak." Shane shrugged. "Is it lame that I have PTSD from that?"

There was a chance that Peter would buy it. That neither of them would be in danger because of his lack of filter.

"No, kids can be cruel. I'm sorry you had to go through that." He paused. "Why did they think you were weak?"

"My size, I guess. And, believe it or not, I was quiet."

He chuckled and shook his head. "I don't believe it."

They should quit while they were ahead. Stop before he said something he'd regret.

"I'm fuckin' exhausted," he slurred his words on purpose. "I should get some sleep."

"Yeah, you should." Peter got up from his seat. "You should also see a doctor."

"Not happening."

"Well, I tried." He shrugged. "I'll be back in the morning to check on you."

4

"Fuck." Shane groaned as he placed his hand to his head.

Looking at the time on his phone, he saw that only an hour had passed since Peter had returned to his own room. He felt weak, nauseated, and lonely. The memories he'd tucked away for the past few years were coming back with a vengeance, and now he couldn't sleep without dreaming them.

When he woke, he often felt sick to his stomach. Nothing made him feel better.

Except for, maybe, one thing.

Swallowing his pride, he scrolled through his contacts until he found Callan's number.

I wish you were here. There, text sent. Simple and to the point.

To his surprise, he received a text back almost instantly. **So do I. But I'm in New York.** There was a sad-face emoji accompanying the statement.

Shane stared at the message to make sure he'd read it correctly before replying. **I'm in New York too. What are the chances?**

Again, a response came with lightning speed. **Where are you?**

This could be it; the turning point in their relationship. If he ignored Cal, lied, or declined, it could set them back or keep them stuck in a rut. But if he let him in, it would show that Shane not only wanted to love, but to be loved as well. And he wanted that, all of it, and yet, he didn't know if he could let himself be happy.

It wasn't that he didn't necessarily think he deserved love, he just didn't think he could keep it. And if he couldn't keep it, what was the point of having it at all?

Against his better judgment, Shane sent Callan the address.

He hadn't realized that he'd dozed off until there was a knock at his door. While he was still tempted to chicken out and ignore the fact that there was a tall, gorgeous man on the other side of that door, he couldn't bear the thought of sleeping alone.

He opened the door and Callan stepped inside.

"You look pale," he spoke quietly. "Even in the dark, I can tell."

"Shut up and kiss me."

Cal didn't act on his command, simply staring at him as if he wasn't sure he'd meant it.

Shane's body was aching for Callan's touch. Even though he knew this was a bad idea, and that they might regret it when the sun rose, he pressed his lips to Cal's.

His fears and doubts melted away, fading into the background like an insignificant detail. Why did this older man have such a calming effect on him? It wasn't fair when he couldn't keep this.

Callan was eagerly exploring Shane's mouth with his tongue, and Shane was happy to return the favor. But as soon as his hands gripped Cal's shirt and tried to lift it up, the older man stopped him.

"We shouldn't."

Looking up at him, Shane furrowed his brow. "Why the fuck not?"

"Because...if we ever go there again, I want it to be special."

"And this isn't special?"

Callan smiled and shook his head. "It's certainly spontaneous and passionate, but it isn't very romantic."

"Mmm." He pursed his lips and folded his arms. "And you want to sweep me off my feet, is that it?"

"It's the least I can do." Callan kissed his forehead. "And you deserve romance."

Now that the mood had been successfully killed, he sighed and walked over to the bed. "You broke character. I want to go back to the game by morning."

"Does that mean I can stay?"

"Yes. Now get over here and spoon me."

Callan did exactly as he was asked. "I don't remember you being this bossy."

"I told you, I've changed."

With Cal's arms around him, Shane drifted off into a comfortable slumber.

The next morning, he woke to a note on the bedside table. Cal had to work but he would be back later, 'if he was okay with that'. Shane didn't know what he wanted yet, so he wasn't going to respond until he did.

He went into the bathroom to shower and get ready for the day. When he got out, there was a figure on his bed and he nearly jumped out of his skin. It was only Peter, but his heart was beating wildly against his rib cage.

"Don't *ever* do that again."

"Try not to have a heart attack, will ya?" Peter raised his brow. "I had no idea you scared so easily."

Swallowing hard, he rubbed his chest, waiting for the discomfort to subside. "I wasn't expecting anyone to be in my room."

"You sure about that?" With a smirk, he gestured to the pillows. "Looks like someone else *was* in your room."

Shane pursed his lips. That wasn't something he wanted to discuss.

"Are you going to spill or what?"

"I'm thinkin' a hard no on that."

"Was it that guy?"

"What guy?"

"*The* guy."

"No," he lied.

"Fine, don't tell me." He raised his hands before rising from the bed. "Let's get something to eat. Looks like you worked up an appetite."

"I didn't-we didn't-" He let out an exasperated sigh. "Not that it's any of your business..."

"Calm down," Pete said with a chuckle. "I'm just giving you a hard time. Not that I would judge."

"Did *you* spend the night alone, mister nosy-pants?"

"I did. But tonight might be a different story."

Peter motioned for Shane to follow him out the door.

Shane was lost in thought for most of the morning. Breakfast was spent making small talk with a story or two of Pete's adventurous evening. Shane was invited to the next night of shenanigans; he had to make a decision about that too.

Callan or shenanigans?

Love and lust or drinking and puking?

To Callan or not to Callan?

He wished someone could make up his mind for him.

The check came and it snapped him out of a daze, though Peter quickly slid his credit card into the folder. Shane's nostrils flared in protest.

"Come on, my treat."

Shane pursed his lips. "I don't know."

"You'll get the next one," he offered.

With a narrowed gaze, he hesitantly nodded. "Okay."

The waiter took the folder away.

Peter lifted his chin, gesturing to Shane. "What's that about anyway?"

He raised an eyebrow. "You got a problem with me wanting to pay for my own things?"

"No. I'm just interested in the reason behind it. This is more than you being offended that I might *assume* you feel just as entitled as the rest of your generation. There's something deeper there."

"I just don't like the feeling of owing someone something. People do that, you know, even if they say they're not keeping track, they are. And if I owe someone something, in a way, they own me. And I don't like feeling as if someone owns me."

Peter's mouth hung open a while before he scoffed. "Your thought process astounds me. You think that when people offer to buy you something, it's because they want you to be indebted to them?"

"When I was younger, people didn't buy me things without wanting something in return. There were always strings attached."

He paused. Something had clicked, Shane could see it in his eyes. "Well, now that makes perfect sense. For future reference, would you prefer I never offer to buy you anything again?"

The question caught him off-guard. No one had bothered to ask before. His family usually simply took offense without hearing him out or offering a solution. "It's not...I mean, sometimes it's okay. Just ask first."

"Got it."

"It's that easy, huh?"

Peter furrowed his brow. "What do you mean?"

He shrugged. "No one ever listens to me."

"I'm here, I've got ears, and I'm interested in whatever you want to say." Peter folded his arms to show his intent to stay a while. "And I would never be nice to you just because I was expecting something in return."

Shane's gaze fell to the table. "That's because you're a good person."

He chuckled deeply. "I'm not a good person, kid."

"Neither am I," he whispered.

"Yeah, you are."

Fidgeting under the table to mask his anxiousness, he cleared his throat. "I'm sure your kid thinks you're okay."

"Guess I'll never know. He was pissed at me when he died."

Shane's gaze snapped to Peter's. "Your kid died?"

He swallowed hard and gave a slow nod. "Yep."

"Jesus, Pete." How had he not known this? Granted, that was the point of this weekend – to get to know each other better. But it was something he should have sensed. It was so strange that Peter didn't carry an air of tragedy about him. How was he able to hide it so well? Almost as well as Shane. "I'm really sorry."

The look in his eyes had changed. No longer playful,

they were dull; they had lost their spark. "I'd like to say time heals all wounds, but it doesn't."

"I know how that goes. Do you want to talk about it?" Running a hand through his hair, the corners of his lips twitched at a smirk. "I'm here, I've got ears, and I'm interested in whatever you want to say."

Peter chuckled and shook his head. "Another time. Let's do fun shit today."

Fun shit consisted of eating, sight-seeing, and walking a lot. It was surprising since he was pretty sure that Peter had a very different idea of the word fun. They both did in a sense, but maybe Peter could see that he was struggling. As usual, he had a bag filled with essentials slung over his shoulder, just in case.

The nosebleeds and nightmares had drained his energy. All he really wanted to do was go back to the room and sleep. Or not sleep at all.

Callan was on his mind, and even though his ex and possibly future lover had suggested they wait, his body was hungry for attention. It would be nice to have a release with all the stress he'd been carrying.

But Cal did have a point. Would sleeping together now cheapen what this was and whatever it might be? For Shane's sake, they were ignoring everything that had gone wrong last time. In fact, they were pretending as if there *hadn't been* a last time. It was easier that way, at least for now. The way he saw it, they could move forward without addressing what had held them back in the past.

Was it the right way to go about this? No. But it was *his* way.

"I haven't seen you touch your phone all day."

"Hmm?" Pulled from his thoughts, Shane looked away

from the fountain in front of them. "I'm not terribly attached to the thing."

"Really?" Peter raised his brow. "There's no one you want to communicate with while you're away?"

"No. It's a weekend." He shrugged. "We're all adults, we all have lives."

"Hmm." The older man eyed him suspiciously. "Okay."

"You have something to say about that?"

"You still talk to your parents, right?"

"One of them. I have a brother too." He paused and pursed his lips. "Where are you going with this?"

"If my kid – adult or not – was gone for a weekend and I didn't hear from him, I would worry." Peter's gaze fell and his voice softened. "But that's probably just because I know how fragile life can be."

"So do I."

"Don't let me guilt you into keeping in touch with your family." He offered a small smile. "Just think about it."

Shane used to have an abundance of empathy for people. It had been some time since he'd tried, but seeing the effect this had on Peter, he couldn't help but reconsider his high walls. Maybe he could lower them, just a little, and be vulnerable for the sake of another person. "I talk to them several times a week. I didn't think a weekend was a big deal, but I'll take that into consideration."

He nodded slowly. "You said you only talk to one of your parents."

"Yeah. I haven't spoken to my dad in years." He clicked his tongue. "I imagine you have something to say about that too."

"Well, of course I do. I assume there's a reason for the strain in your relationship, but I can relate to that situation."

So that was the reason for this conversation. He was

projecting. That was fine, Shane couldn't fault him for that because he had no idea what it was like to lose a child. However, the situation with his father couldn't be compared to Peter's relationship with his son. At least, he hoped not. "Listen, I don't know why your son was mad at you. But I can assure you that there are very good reasons for the strain in the relationship between my father and me."

"Okay, I won't push." He raised his hands defensively. "It's just a very sad thing when families become distant. Life happens, tragedy happens, and it doesn't wait for us to get our shit together."

Shane swallowed the lump in his throat. He was going to have nightmares for sure. The older man needn't tell him about life and tragedy; he knew that fact quite well from his own experiences. "Pete, I'm really sorry about you and your son. But I'm asking you never to speak about my father again."

Peter was silent. His gaze wandered over the shorter brunette, sizing him up before nodding. "Heard loud and clear."

Now the silence was mutual. All of his physical and emotional energy had been sucked dry. It had been quite some time since he'd spent a day, or a weekend, with someone – relative, friend, or otherwise.

"Want to try my idea of fun?" came Peter's voice.

He raised an eyebrow. "Is that your way of saying you've been bored all day?"

"On the contrary, I've had a wonderful time and don't want it to end, which is why I'm trying to extend it."

"Oh." He'd never heard that before. It was nice to hear that someone enjoyed his company. "Well, I'd like to. Is there any chance we could make it an early night though? I might have plans later."

"I see, hot shot." Peter nudged him. "Don't worry, you can leave any time your heart desires. We'll call you a cab."

"Or I can walk." He shrugged. "I don't mind."

"Whatever you want to do. Come on, I know a place."

"I'm not surprised."

Following Peter to their next destination, Shane's mind wandered to his family. His boss had given him a lot to think about and it made him question why he was tagging along. Maybe he was just trying to be polite. What he really wanted to do was call his mother.

He was pulled from his thoughts when they entered a strip club. It wasn't a place he'd ever thought he would be with his boss, but this wasn't something he was going to complain about.

"It's really high-end," Peter assured him as they walked over to a group of men.

"I'll take your word for it."

Now was he really regretting his decision. This wasn't something he was comfortable with, being in a situation with a bunch of people that Peter knew, and he did not.

"Who's this?" one of them asked. "Your new boy toy?"

"He's not my type," Peter said with a chuckle.

Shane scrunched his nose. "Yeah, I'm too short."

"I like you already." The man laughed before introducing himself as well as the rest of the group. "Name's Jamie. This is Trent, Alvin, and Corey." They looked harmless enough, though that didn't mean much in today's world. "Can we get you something to drink?"

He shook his head. "No, thanks."

Alvin jerked his thumb in Peter's direction. "How can you handle this guy when you're sober?"

"Who said I was sober?" His answer brought laughter from all but Peter.

"Touché!" Corey said with a nod. "Well, not to worry, you're in good company."

"That's...questionable."

"Wow." Trent looked between him and Peter. "If I didn't know any better, Pete, I'd say he was a chip off the ol' block!"

"Yeah." Peter clapped Shane on the back. "He reminds me of a younger, though not as good-looking, me."

"Jeez," Alvin mumbled, "Take it easy on him."

"Are you kidding me? He gives just as good as he gets." Peter turned to Shane, raising his brow. "Sometimes better."

Shane clicked his tongue. "Gosh, Pete, coming from you, that means absolutely nothing."

"Okay, this is freaking me out." Trent raised his hands. "Are you sure you two aren't related?"

"I'm pretty sure." Peter winked at Shane. "The kid can thank his lucky stars for that."

"My unlucky stars, more like," Shane spoke softly, barely audible over the noise of the club. "I could do worse."

It was a statement that seemed to shocked everyone, none of them able to muster a response. Before the silence lingered for an unbearably awkward amount of time, Shane cast his gaze elsewhere, pretending to be interested in the women dancing on various poles.

What caught his eye was not a woman at all, but a tall, devastatingly handsome blond man.

Callan.

For a moment, he thought he might be able to sneak out of the club unnoticed, and then good ol' Cal locked eyes with him, and it was all over.

Shane smiled and waved before leaving the group of men to be with the one he favored above all others.

"Shane!" Callan was beaming. "Fancy meeting you here."

"I should have text you." He slid his hands into his pockets to hide his fidgeting. "Sorry about that, I've had a busy day."

Callan looked toward the group of men that Shane had come from, nodding slowly. "So I see."

"It's not like that."

"It wouldn't be my business if it was, right?"

"Right." Shane pursed his lips, wanting so badly to tell him what it was. He wasn't sure it mattered. "So, what brings you here? The food?"

"Yes, actually." He laughed and they walked over to a tank that was placed near the entrance. "My friends have other plans, but I'm here for the best lobster in town."

"Are you?" His gaze wandered over the tank. The poor lobster were squished, too crowded in the tank. He wondered if they had room to breathe, room to feel, room to wonder what was going to happen to them. "I could never eat them. It's alive and then you decide you want to eat it. Then it gets tortured for you to have your meal."

Cal raised his brow. "Are you a vegetarian?"

"I want to be." Shane swallowed hard. "I can't handle cruelty."

"So why aren't you?"

He paused. "It's better for my health if I'm not. High doses of iron are good for me."

Callan tilted his head. "Are you okay, Shane?"

Blinking rapidly as if it would make his worries disappear, he nodded. "Yeah, why do you ask?"

"You don't seem okay," he spoke softly. "Do you want some company tonight?"

With the memories swirling around his mind, that probably wasn't a good idea. If there was one thing he hated, it was being vulnerable. He might slip up and say something he hadn't intended to, all because he was feeling sensitive.

As much as he wanted to feel the warmth and comfort of Callan's arms around him, he couldn't justify it.

"I think I'd prefer the lobster."

That was mean. It had been unnecessary and the complete opposite of what he really meant. Shane just couldn't help himself. That was no way to recover from that except to apologize, though apologizing also expressed vulnerability, the very thing he was trying so desperately to avoid.

"See you around," he mumbled.

Needing a moment of peace and quiet, Shane walked past Peter and his merry band of men and went into the bathroom. He could still hear the thumping of the music on the other side of the door, but at least no one was going to bother him in there.

Moving his bag from his shoulder to his hand, Shane dug inside for a bottle, long overdue for his medication. As repulsive as it was to take it there, he couldn't help his natural impulse to be secretive. He didn't want Callan or Peter to know about his condition, refusing to appear weak in front of anyone. After plopping the pills into his mouth, he scooped the less-than-desirable sink water into his hand and swallowed them.

When he turned around, Peter was staring at him, brow raised. "I assume there's a perfectly reasonable explanation for this too."

Shane ran his tongue over his front teeth. "There is."

"Out with it."

He scoffed. "I'm not obligated to tell you."

"Come on, kid. First the nosebleed, now this. I think I'm owed an explanation."

His nostrils flared and jaw clenched. "I don't owe you a fucking thing."

"You're right. Keep your secrets." He raised his hands defensively before turning around, heading for the door. "Let me know if we're still traveling together tomorrow."

For the sake of their growing personal relationship, Shane wanted to be honest. He was going to swallow his pride and share something he would rather not because, contrary to popular belief, he gave a shit. "Can we not have this conversation here? I don't want you to cut your night short but-"

"Don't worry about my nights, I have plenty of them." Peter opened the door and gestured for Shane to walk through it. "If you want to talk, let's talk."

He tried to look for Callan on his way out, but he was nowhere to be found, so Shane had no choice but to leave without saying goodbye.

Having to be vulnerable made him nervous and his palms were clammy. He rehearsed what he was going to say in his mind, not speaking a word until they were in Peter's room. It was much cleaner than his.

Clearing his throat, Shane tossed his bag to the older man, who caught it with both hands. "I was diagnosed with hypertrophic cardiomyopathy at sixteen, which eventually led to heart failure and a heart attack at twenty. I'm lucky if I live to see thirty."

Peter opened the bag to check the medication. "You were twenty? Jesus Christ, kid."

"Yeah. Life's a bitch and then you die." He shrugged. "There are medications, surgeries, transplants – all that fun shit and still, patients like me only live ten years on average. No matter what, I'm on medication for life and looking at multiple transplants to live a quote-unquote *normal* life."

He was silent for what seemed like an eternity. Then he heaved a sigh and handed Shane the bag. "Why didn't you just tell me?"

"Because I don't like people knowing that I'm weak." It was an admission he hadn't been prepared to make. Admitting weakness was a *sign* of weakness; that was what he'd been taught.

Peter's gaze wandered over him, head shaking slowly. "You're anything but weak. In fact, I think you're *too* strong. But I understand what you mean because I've become the same way. We hide our pain so that we can deny just how deeply it hurts."

Shane made his way to the door. "I don't want anyone to think I'm using my condition as an excuse to be a dick."

"I don't think that. And I'm certainly not using the death of my child as an excuse for my behavior. It's just easier to be angry, isn't it?"

Finally, someone understood. He nodded. "I'm pretty tired, so I'm going to call it a night."

"Get some rest. We can go back to being assholes in the morning."

Shane laughed before opening the adjoining door to enter his room. But as soon as he closed it, he heard a knock on the other door. When he looked through the peephole, he was surprised to see Callan standing there. Though, as he opened the door, he tried not to seem shocked at all. The taller man was standing with a small tank in his hands and a very live lobster inside it.

"What is this?" he asked with a furrowed brow.

"My lobster." Callan held out the tank to him.

"Um...what?"

He moved aside so that Cal could come in. The tank was set on the table and Shane closed the door.

"I ordered a lobster to go," Cal said as he stepped away from the tank. "Uncooked. I saved its life for you."

Shane's jaw dropped, his gaze moving from the lobster in the tank to the unbelievably beautiful man in front of him. "That's...wow." Tears came to his eyes, but since he hadn't turned on the light, Cal wouldn't be able to see. Still, his voice broke when he said, "Thank you, Cal."

"I'm taking him to professionals tomorrow. Hopefully, he'll be released. Or live a long life in an aquarium. Either way, he'll live."

He swallowed hard, afraid that he already knew the answer, but wanting to ask anyway. "Do you want to stay?"

Callan shook his head with a chuckle. "If I had known that was all it would take, I would have rescued a lobster years ago!"

Throwing his arms around the much taller man, Shane pulled him closer, pressing their bodies together. "Just hold me. I need you."

"Okay, Shane," he spoke quietly, enveloping Shane in his arms. Cal's chin rested on the top of his head. "All this because I saved a lobster? You're so sweet. You know that?"

"No. I have a reputation for being prickly. Like a cactus."

"My own little cactus." He grinned, pulling away to look at Shane's face. "That is adorable."

Shane paused, looking right back into Callan's eyes. "You know how a cactus gets those little flowers sometimes?"

"Yeah, sure."

"Mine will bloom only for you."

He closed his eyes, shaking his head. "You can't say things like that to me."

Shane furrowed his brow. "Why not?"

"Because I..." Dipping his chin, his gaze faltered. "I want you. So very much."

"Hmm." Shane's hands slipped underneath Cal's shirt, slowly sliding up his back. "We'll have to do something about that, won't we?"

In what seemed like seconds, they had done away with their clothing, and were thrashing around on the bed. They succumbed to sleep when the sun began to shine through the window.

5

It was hours later that Shane woke. Callan was absent from the bed and he could hear the shower running. He stretched and got to his feet, hoping to join his lover in the shower. Alas, just as he was heading in, Callan walked out.

"You couldn't wait for me to join you?"

"You've never let me see you shirtless, Shane. I didn't think today would be any different." Cal smiled and kissed him gently. "And I didn't want to wake you. I assumed you would want to sleep in."

He raised his brow. "You weren't going to leave without saying goodbye, were you?"

"Come on. After last night, do you really think I'd do that?"

He shrugged and mumbled, "You've left me before."

"That's never going to happen again." Cal's lips pressed to Shane's, hands roaming his body before one gave his ass a squeeze. "But I do need to head home. Maybe you can meet me there...or better yet, come with me?"

"I came with you this morning, didn't I?" He smirked

when seeing the blush on Cal's cheeks. "I should head back with Peter. Who is my boss, by the way."

"You don't owe me an explanation." He paused, tilting his head. "Can I ask you a question?"

"You just did," he responded with a chuckle.

"Why won't you let me see you without a shirt?"

Shane moved out of his arms and toward the sink. He squeezed minty paste onto his toothbrush and brushed his teeth, Cal eyeing him all the while. "I just don't like being that exposed. I've always been that way, nothing's changed."

"Yes, it has." He wrapped his arms around the smaller man, placing a kiss on the back of his head. "Or are we still not discussing that?"

"Nope." Shane was quick to slip away, turning on the shower.

"Will you tell me when you're ready?"

"Nope." Pursing his lips, he turned back to Callan. He realized that he was being cold, and if he wasn't careful, he would push Cal away. Although that would have been best for both of them, Shane couldn't help being a little selfish. "I'll call you when we land. I want to make plans for next weekend."

"Haven't you had enough of me yet?"

Shane stepped forward, gripped his hips, and kissed him softly. "Not nearly."

The sweetest smile that Shane had ever seen spread across Callan's cheeks. "Good."

He took his shower in private and then gave Callan a proper goodbye before he left. Shane packed his bags and heard a knock on the door, though he didn't give permission before Peter entered.

The older man scrunched his nose. "Smells like sex in here."

"That's probably because I had sex in here."

"Oh?" He folded his arms. "And this person's name is..."

Shane rolled his eyes. "None of your business."

"That's a strange name." He narrowed his gaze. "Could it be the handsome fellow from last night? The guy you told me about at the shop?"

"Yes," he said with an exasperated sigh. "It was Callan. Are you happy now?"

"Well, look at you! Opening up to people and all. I'm so proud."

Shane swung one bag over his shoulder and pulled his suitcase by the handle. "We fucked. That's all."

Peter raised his brow. "He doesn't know, does he?"

"Nope."

"You don't plan on telling him, do you?"

"Nope."

"Hmm." Peter's gaze wandered over him. "I thought you loved him."

"What does that have to do with anything?"

"Because you don't lie to the people you love."

Shane's nostrils flared. "You do if it keeps them safe."

He furrowed his brow. "And while you're busy protecting everyone else, who's protecting you?"

Grinding his teeth, he shook his head. "No one."

"Because you won't let them."

"Because I can't." Letting the bag over his should drop to his side, Shane walked toward the door. "Look, you wouldn't understand."

"I might if you gave me a chance."

"No, I mean, you don't understand what *telling* you would mean." He opened the door, keeping it ajar with his foot. "Just leave it alone, if not for your sake then for mine."

· · ·

HIS MOTHER HAD BEEN DOING HER BEST TO MAKE HIM FEEL welcome. She was struggling to keep her faith as well as her son, and while he wished that the answer could have been simple, he knew that it wasn't. Not for his mother. And if she could try to understand him then he could do the same for her.

He walked into her house, the very one he'd grown up in, and was greeted with the smell of baked pasta. "What is that?"

"I made your favorite!" Lorraine called from the kitchen.

Shane walked inside and stood against the counter. "You didn't have to make lasagna just for me."

"Anything for my boy." She smiled and pinched his cheek.

"Do you still make dinner for Ethan?"

"Sometimes I'll go over and cook with him. Or play with the kids while he and Nora cook." Using a pair of oven mitts, she moved the hot pan onto the dinner table. "Do you spend a lot of time with them?"

He grabbed two plates and two forks from the cabinets and then sat down next to her. "I try to, but I don't really get along with Nora. And she doesn't get along with me."

She clicked her tongue. "You two should give each other a chance. You're family."

"It's okay if we don't like each other." He shrugged. "As long as I get to spend time with Ethan and the kids, that's all that matters."

"Well, I won't get in the middle of you three. You're all adults, you can figure it out."

Using the serving spoon, he put a large piece of lasagna on each of their plates. "How was your weekend?"

"Uneventful. I just did some cleaning, caught up on some shows. How was yours?"

He raised his brow. "Do you really want to know?"

"Of course I do."

"Even if I spent it with a guy?"

She paused and tilted her head. "I won't lie, it's something I'm still getting used to. But what makes my boys happy makes me happy, so...tell me everything."

He smirked. "Well, I won't tell you *everything*."

"Oh," she said with a nervous giggle. "The weekend went that well, huh?"

"It was unexpected, for the both of us, I think." Color flushed his cheeks as he shifted in his seat. "Do you remember when I told you about Callan?"

"Yes." She nodded slowly. "He was your first love, if I remember correctly."

He blinked rapidly, surprised that she had, indeed, remembered. "You really were listening."

She pouted her lip and ran a hand through his curls. "I'm sorry if you thought I wasn't. I am trying, honey. I have been. And I deeply regret that you had to keep your relationship with him a secret. I should have been there for you and I wasn't, but I am now."

"I know it's not easy for you." He gave a small smile. "I appreciate it."

"So, what does Callan have to do with your weekend?"

"Apparently, he's back in town. And, to make a long story short, I went to New York on a last-minute trip. And Callan just happened to be there too." He shrugged. "It was like fate or something."

"Does that mean you two are back together?"

"I don't know," he mumbled, poking his lasagna. "We haven't put a label on it."

"So you still haven't forgiven him for breaking your heart."

She had remembered that too? Shane was impressed, though it put a damper on his favorite meal. "I guess not. I'm trying to because I really want to be with him."

She waved her fork in his direction. "Have you had an honest conversation about how it affected you?"

"No."

"Then why did you take your relationship to the next level?"

He clicked his tongue and shifted uncomfortably. He should have expected his mother to give him the third degree, but that was alright, it was better than ignoring the situation altogether. "We're kind of...pretending that none of that stuff ever happened."

Lorraine sighed and shook her head. "That's no good, Shane. You can't have a relationship of any kind like that."

"I know. I'm working on it." His mother took a few bites in silence, as did he, though his mind wasn't blank. If ever there was a time to ask her this question, it was now. "Can I ask you something kinda personal?"

She set down her fork. "You can ask me anything."

He paused, hoping it wouldn't make her uncomfortable. "Have you dated anyone since...dad?"

She smiled softly and touched his hand. "I've been on a few dates. But, as you know, my relationships with Ethan's father, and then yours, didn't end well. And they were the only men I'd ever been with. Since they were both bad experiences, I decided to give up on love and just focus on raising you boys."

Growing up, he hadn't given much thought to his mother's personal happiness. He'd been preoccupied with a plethora of teenage problems and hadn't stopped to think about how it might affect his mother. "I don't want you to be alone."

"I'm not alone, honey." Lorraine leaned over and kissed his cheek. "I never will be."

CLEARING HIS THROAT, SHANE OPENED A DOOR TO THE entrance of the mall, allowing Ethan to walk in first. "Thanks for meeting up with me."

"Sure." Shoving his hands in his pockets, he walked beside his brother. "Sorry I'm not much help, I don't know Nora very well."

"I just wanted the company." Ethan shrugged. "Mom said you went on a trip?"

"Yeah."

"You should have told someone."

He raised an eyebrow. "Why, are you worried I'll drop dead?"

"Yes."

Shaking his head, he heaved a sigh. "It was just a weekend, everything was fine. How's the bar coming along?"

"The remodeling is going very well." He paused. "So, you had a good time?"

"Yeah, it was fun."

It was Ethan's turn to hold the door open as they walked into a store. "Did you smile at all?"

He clicked his tongue. "Maybe once."

"Because of Callan?"

Shane wasn't sure how to feel about that. On one hand, it was nice that they could talk about these things. On the other, he wasn't sure he wanted to. "Great, mom told you."

"I was hoping *you'd* tell me, Shane," his voice was low and deep. "But you never talk to me."

"We're talking now. I always talk to you, Ethan. I just don't want to discuss my personal life."

He sighed as he flicked through several blouses on a rack. "You're my brother, and I love you, but I've never felt close to you because you've always had your guard up."

Shane furrowed his brow. "Wow, you don't think we're close?"

"Come on." Ethan shot him a look before moving on to the next rack of clothing. "You know everything about my life and I never get to know what's happening in yours."

"That's not true. I told you about Callan."

"Yeah, two years after you broke up."

"Well, mom was still toxic when I was with Callan, so I didn't want to tell you."

He nodded slowly. "That's fair, I suppose. But I wouldn't have cared, you know."

That was easy to say now, after the fact, but they couldn't have known that then. "Uh-huh."

"So," he drawled, "Are you going to tell me about him?"

"No." He pursed his lips, following Ethan to the shoe section of the store. "It's complicated."

"It always is with you." He shook his head. "At least you're normal today."

Shane folded his arms. "Define *normal*."

"Oh, don't start." He rolled his eyes. "We were getting along so nicely."

His gaze narrowed as Ethan held up two different pairs of shoes – one being red boots and the other being pink, sparkly high-heels. "The boots seem more like Nora's taste."

SHANE'S GAZE WAS FIXED ON THE CEILING. CAL'S LOFT WAS like a palace compared to his dinky apartment. He didn't feel comfortable there. Everything had a place, the floors and counters were spotless, and all the knick-knacks looked like they belonged in a museum.

He understood that Cal, more than likely, had a maid to keep the place so tidy, but it made him wonder how he fit in and why Cal would be interested in someone like him.

His apartment was a representation of who he was as a person – rough and tattered. Cal's loft was stunning and refined, just like the man himself.

Who was Shane to bring such chaos into Callan's organized life?

Callan nuzzled his neck, hand casually lifting the bottom of Shane's shirt. "What are you hiding under there, hmm?"

"Nothing." He tugged it down and slapped Cal's hand.

"And under here?" Gently gripping Shane's hip, his thumb rubbed over the bandage that seemed to reside there permanently.

"Nothing." The hand in question was slapped again.

He took the hint and let go. "I can't believe I've never seen you completely naked."

"I just like having sex with my clothes on."

"Or in the dark." Over the shirt, his hand crawled up to Shane's chest. "Which is very difficult to navigate at times, might I add."

"I know, I'm very particular." He wrapped his arm around Cal's back. "Is that a problem for you?"

"It never has been." He paused. "Will you ever let me make love to you?"

"No." His body tensed when Cal placed a hand on his cheek and trailed soft kisses along his neck. "Stop it, Cal. Don't push your luck."

Rolling onto his back, he heaved a sigh. "Do you have any idea what it's like to be with you?"

"Why don't you tell me?"

"Sometimes you're wonderful and I know exactly how you feel. Other times, you're cold." He shook his head. "I feel alone even though you're right next to me."

Shane sat up, propping the pillows before leaning against them. "I'm sorry, Cal. I don't mean to be cold. I want you all the time." He offered the older man his hand, and when Cal took it, he interlaced their fingers. "Sex is a distraction for me. I get lost in it. But as soon as it's over...you want to hold me, touch me, caress me. It's steady, gentle motions that I can't handle. It's like an over-stimulation for me, being *too* gentle." He shrugged. "With sex, you keep moving."

Cal rested his back against his pillow, now close to eye-level with Shane. "I'm sorry, I didn't know that."

"No, *I'm* sorry." He leaned over and placed a kiss on his lips. "I know you need that gentleness, that affection. I want to give that to you, it's just...it's difficult."

"I don't need anything, just you." He brushed his thumb over Shane's knuckles. "Can I ask you why it's like that for you?"

He considered ignoring the question or simply not answering it. There was a small part of him that wanted to run, like always, and avoid the subject completely. And then he could regroup and come back when he'd stuffed those feelings down, like always. But he knew that if he wanted Callan to stay, and he did, he had to let down his walls. At least a little bit. "I was handled with a lot of brutality in the past. So when someone is gentle with me, when someone is nice, I can't accept it. I don't know what to do with it, so I reject it."

"Does that mean you hate lying with me like this?"

"No, it's – sometimes I'm okay with it, as long as I don't think about it too much."

He brought Shane's hand to his lips. "So what should I do?"

"You've been perfect. I just..." He swallowed hard. "If I turn away, or if I can't handle you touching me softly, it's not because I don't care about you. I don't want you to feel like I'm using you, or-"

"Shane, it's okay." Cal silenced him with a kiss. "You've explained yourself, so now I understand. I'll give you space when you need it. And I'll be here when you do want my affection."

Shane stared into Cal's twinkling blue eyes. They were so kind and genuine. He'd never seen another pair of eyes like his. "I don't deserve you."

"Whatever happened to make you this way, I just want you to know that you don't ever have to tell me. I will love you regardless. I may not always understand, but I will never, ever, leave you over this."

He furrowed his brow. Even though he had already guessed as much, the word still surprised him. "You love me?"

"I do. And you don't have to say it back. I just wanted you to know."

Shane didn't know how he felt about that. Any normal person would have wanted that all along, but Shane was not a normal person. This was not a normal relationship. He was trying so very hard to pretend that it was, but, eventually, he knew that he would have to let Callan go.

Just as he closed his eyes to drift off to sleep, his cell phone rang. With a groan, he reached across his lover and grabbed the phone from the bedside table.

"Peter?"

"Who is this?" came a slurred voice from the other end.

"Um...it's Shane."

"Oh, hey, man. What's up?"

"You're the one who called *me*."

"Oh, right."

Shane furrowed his brow. He could hear loud music in the background and several people laughing. "Are you drunk?"

"Maybe just a smidge."

Heaving a sigh, he rolled out of bed. "Okay, where are you?"

"I'm at this little bar. I think it's called Jake's. Isn't that funny?"

"Why would that be funny?"

"I don't know, it's a weird name for a bar."

Shane slipped on his jeans over his boxers and then tugged on his shoes one-handed. "I'm on my way. Just stay put. Can you do that?"

"I think I can manage that. The room is kinda spinning so I can't really go anywhere."

He ended the call and grabbed his backpack from the chair in the corner of the room. "I have to go, babe. It's my boss."

"Promise you'll stay the night next time?"

"Promise." Shane leaned down and kissed Callan's soft lips before heading out of the apartment.

Luckily for him, there weren't a hell of a lot of bars called Jake's, and only one remotely close to Peter's neighborhood.

Once he arrived, he hurried into the bar and found his friend slumped over a table.

"Pete, let's go." Shane gently grabbed his arm. "We have work in the morning."

"Work shmerk." He sat up and tugged his arm away. "Take the day off. In fact, take a week off!"

He furrowed his brow. "Are you firing me?"

"No, I'm encouraging you to get a life. Something wrong with that?"

"Yeah, you're insinuating that I don't have one."

"Well, *I* don't."

Shane chewed his bottom lip anxiously, wondering how he was going to drag the man out of there. Hearing footsteps behind them, he turned to see a large, burly man with a beer in his hand.

"Get out of here, child killer. Before we throw you out."

Peter got to his feet, his hands balled into fists. "What did you say to me?"

"Whoa, Peter, don't engage." Shane moved in between them, hand held up to keep them separated. "Let it go."

"Yeah, listen to the little faggot."

Peter shoved Shane aside and lunged for the burly stranger. "Don't call him that!"

"Pete, it's not worth it!" He attempted to get in between them again, but the stranger pushed him with such force that he fell to the floor.

The two men exchanged punches before the bartender threatened to call the police. That was the last thing they needed, so Shane carefully stood up, checking his clothes for any signs of blood.

"Shane, are you okay?" Peter placed a hand on his shoulder. "Shane?"

"I'm fine."

"Are you bleeding?"

"No, but you are." Slinging one of Peter's arms around his neck, Shane helped him out of the bar and into his vehicle. "You got your keys?"

"Yeah, here."

Shane took the set from his boss and locked Peter's car before shoving them into his pocket. "You'll have to pick that up tomorrow."

Once they were both safely inside Shane's car, he headed in the direction of Peter's house. He helped the older man up the steps to the porch and then inside setting him on the couch. "What was that about anyway?"

Peter took in a shaky breath. "People think I killed my kid."

"What?" Shane folded his arms. "Why do they think that?"

"People always look at the parents when a kid goes missing." Head hung low so that Shane couldn't see his tears, he sniffled. "I miss him, Shane. I miss him so fucking much. I'm all alone."

"You're not alone, you've got me."

He shook his head and wiped his eyes with his sleeve. "You're a good man, Shane Coulter."

Shane helped him lie on his side before sticking a pillow under his head and then covering him with a blanket. "No, I'm not."

"Yes, you are," Peter whispered.

6

He was so tired, so preoccupied, that he'd considered canceling. Since time with his family was limited, he knew that he needed to take advantage when he could. But now that he was seated across from Ethan and Nora, sharing their meal, Shane realized that he should have stayed home. There was too much on his mind.

"So, Shane, what do you do for a living?"

Nora's question pulled him from his thoughts. "I'm a part-time pain in the ass."

Ethan clicked his tongue. "I think you mean full-time."

"Hey, no one asked you."

He chuckled and shrugged. "I'm just telling it like it is."

With a roll of his eyes, he turned to Nora. "I work at a stone and gem shop. The boss is cool, he's never given me any grief. And it leaves me enough time for my writing...if I ever get back into it."

Nora spooned mashed potatoes onto his plate. "Do you ever want to be more?"

Shane tilted his head from side to side, giving it some

thought. "I wouldn't mind having a best-seller someday, but I'm content where I am."

She handed him a plate of roast beef. "So if you never make it as an author, you don't have a back-up plan?"

"No, like I said, I'm happy where I am." Even though her tone was pleasant, Shane couldn't help feeling that the words were condescending. Being that they were coming from his sister-in-law, he tried to let it go, putting a few slices of meat on his plate before giving it to Ethan.

"You said content," she said pointedly, "Not happy."

"What would you suggest I do, Nora?" He folded his arms. "Please, tell me how I should change my life to be more acceptable by your standards."

Ethan furrowed his brow. "Shane, don't be so hostile."

"*I'm* being hostile? She's insulting me and I'm just supposed to sit back and take it?"

Nora shook her head, her tone unchanged. "I didn't mean to offend you. I was just curious."

"No, you were interrogating me." Shane scrunched his nose. "Cops can't help themselves even outside of work."

She heaved a sigh. "That's another thing, what is it with you and cops?"

"It's nothing against you. It just so happens that I don't like them."

"How can that be?" Nora paused as if to consider her next words carefully. "Isn't your father one?"

He threw a glare in her direction. "What the fuck would you know about my father?"

Ethan slapped his hand on the table. "Shane, that's enough. You're not going to speak to my wife that way."

He scoffed. "Then tell her to lay off!"

Without finishing the meal, Nora collected her plate and

cup. "It was great to see you Shane, as always. We won't be needing you to babysit this weekend. Change of plans."

She walked into the kitchen, leaving the two men in the dining room.

"Yeah, I'm sure," he mumbled.

Ethan shook his head slowly, his features showing his disgust. "What the fuck is wrong with you, Shane? You just can't let alone get close, can you? You're lucky the kids are out tonight."

"I never would have talked that way in front of them. I doubt Nora would have been grilling me if they were here anyway."

While his brother went after his wife, Shane took in a deep, frustrated breath. He couldn't help it; he and Nora just didn't get along. Maybe it was because she was a cop, and he hated them, but maybe not. Either way, he was fully prepared to take the blame for all of the tension. He was just sorry that it was going to cost him time with his niece and nephew.

Picking up his backpack from the floor, he swung it over his shoulder and walked out. It was better to cool off than risk escalating the situation. If they weren't going to see eye to eye, the best thing to do was walk away.

Shane went home to his empty apartment. He had a few beers, a big no-no for him, but sometimes he had to let loose. Especially when he felt like a total fuck-up.

There was a knock on the door, and, as per usual when there was an unexpected visitor, he rushed to hide the variety of pill bottles on his counter before answering it.

"Oh. Hey, Troy."

The slightly taller man with wavy brown hair stepped into the apartment and Shane closed the door.

"So, what brings you by?"

"I don't know." Troy shrugged. "Life. Had a feeling I should stop by, I guess." In a usual friend-fashion, he walked over to the refrigerator and helped himself to a snack. "What's the latest?"

"I'm not getting along with my brother." He leaned against the counter. "Or his wife."

"Shane the Pain living up to his name." Troy closed the refrigerator, a chunk of cheese in his hand. "I assume that's on account of your winning personality."

"Guess so." He scrunched his nose while watching his friend feast on cheese. "How come it doesn't bother *you*?"

"I don't know. Because you're my friend and I'm happy to take you as you are."

"Well...you don't know what I was like before."

"I'm sure that has something to do with it." Troy licked his lips after swallowing a bite. "Anything else on your mind?"

He paused, contemplating whether or not to speak. "Yeah. Cal."

"Talk to me, man." He gestured to Shane with the last bit of cheese in his hand. "What's going on?"

"I don't know if I'm good enough for him now."

"Now?"

"Now that I'm different."

"Well, like you said, I didn't know you before, so I didn't know him or anyone else you've been with. However, you've told me about all of them."

Shane chewed his bottom lip anxiously. "And?"

"And...it sounds like he's the love of your life." Popping the cube into his mouth, he then folded his arms. "After the way your relationship ended the last time, he probably doesn't think he's good enough for *you*. But if the two of you want to be together, I don't see why you'd let anything stand in your way."

If only that were true. If only it were that easy. If only things were that *simple*. "There are so many things..."

Troy furrowed his brow. "What do you mean?"

He shook his head, licking his lips. "I can't tell you."

"Fine, keep your secrets." He raised his hands. "But you should listen to me because I'm your friend, and even if I don't know everything in your past, I still know *you*."

Troy stared at the counter a little too long. For a moment, Shane thought he'd left one of his pill bottles out in the open. Thankfully, it seemed as though his friend had just been gathering his thoughts because he continued.

"It's simple, Shane. If you love him, be with him. If you don't, let him go. Just don't take people for granted, they won't always be around."

"Yeah, that's what I'm worried about." He rolled his eyes. "And this is starting to sound more like a lecture and less like advice."

"You're worried that people will inevitably leave you, so you push them away until they *want* to leave you." Troy nudged him. "You're a cliché, man."

"I appreciate your honesty, dickhead."

"Hey, what are friends for?" As he headed for the front door, he shouted, "Now get the fuck out of here and go be with your man. Thanks for the cheese!"

It took Shane several long minutes to text Callan and invite him over. He always thought it was a bad idea because the more time they spent together, the more he wanted to confide in him. That was what normal couples did.

But they were not a normal couple. Shane couldn't call Callan his boyfriend, couldn't even admit that they were seeing each other.

When he heard the knock, he opened the door, allowing Cal inside without saying a word.

Cal raised his brow, shutting the door with his foot. "Are you drunk?"

"No, just tired." He rubbed his eyes while walking over to the couch. "I wanted to talk to you."

"About what?"

"Anything." After taking a seat, he invited Cal to join him. "How's your relationship with your family?"

Slowly sitting beside him, Cal furrowed his brow. "Uh...fine, I guess."

"Now that you've given up on your dream to be a journalist, you mean?"

"I haven't given up. I just shifted my priorities."

"You gave up everything you cared about in order to please your daddy." He shook his head. "What a cliché."

Cal looked him up and down. "And you're not? I haven't heard a word about *your* father. Judging by your behavior, I'd say you were stuck in your rebellious stage, which is also a cliché."

"If that was supposed to hurt, it didn't. I'm perfectly comfortable with myself."

"That makes one of us," Cal mumbled.

Shane shifted to his side. "What do you mean?"

"Sometimes I can't stand myself, Shane. I'm not comfortable in my own skin. I don't like myself." He heaved a sigh, blinking away tears. "And you're right, I'm not even my own person. I'm exactly who my parents wanted me to be."

"Not with me, you're not," he spoke in a soft tone.

"I'm only my true self when I'm with you."

Shane closed the distance between them by placing a soft kiss on his lips. "I'm sorry if I hurt your feelings. I'm on a roll tonight."

"How so?"

"My brother is pissed at me. He doesn't like my attitude and neither does my sister-in-law." He wiped a hand over his brow. "I just hope it doesn't cost me my relationship with my niece and nephew."

Callan paused, chewing his bottom lip. "Is this because of me?"

"Is what because of you?"

"The way you are."

He swallowed hard. "No. It isn't because of you."

"Then what is it?"

Shane took in a shaky breath. "I can't."

"Will you ever tell me?"

"I don't know." He shrugged. "Maybe someday."

Callan took Shane's hand in his. "So your brother's pissed at you. Are you two close?"

"I like to think so. He's older than me, so he's always been a step ahead, you know? He's always known what he wants out of life. We were being raised at different times and by different people. We have different fathers, you see."

"How did you navigate that?"

"Well, Ethan's father was far removed from the picture by the time I came around. And since Ethan already had a father, he didn't really want anything to do with mine." He paused to chew on his bottom lip. "My father was married to our mother, but Ethan's father never was. I saw my dad every other weekend and Ethan saw his dad on the same weekends I was away. His dad passed away when Ethan was eighteen."

"And your father didn't step in?"

"No. I mean, they were friendly. My dad invited Ethan out with us a few times. But Ethan was grown, he didn't really need more parenting." Shane gave a shrug. "Besides, he had my mom."

He nodded slowly. "Your dad sounds like a nice guy."

"Yeah, that's what everyone says."

"What do *you* say?"

"I say..." Shane leaned over and kissed his neck, his hand working its way underneath Cal's shirt. "Let's stop talking about my family."

He gently pushed him back. "Shane, you can't use sex as a coping mechanism to get out of these conversations."

"Yes, I can, I have, and I will."

"What's your relationship like with your mother?"

With an exasperated sigh, he returned to his seat. "When do you mean?"

"Whenever."

"During my childhood, she thought it was great. But I kept a lot of secrets from her. She relied heavily on her religion to make her feel better about her life choices. Having Ethan out of wedlock and then her marriage to my father ending in divorce...it weighed on her, I guess." He folded his arms. "See, I think when people don't like themselves, they hate other people. She was very homophobic, close-minded. It was bad for my health."

"Your mental health, you mean?"

"Yeah, sure." He was willing to open up, but he had his limits. That was one of them, at least for now. "I was twenty when I told her that I was bisexual. She freaked out at first, but she's really come around since then. I was able to talk to her about a lot of things that I couldn't before. Even told her about my first love."

"And what about your next love? Were you able to tell her about that one, assuming it was a man?"

And they had hit another limit. For the sake of continuing

their charade, Shane had to stop the conversation there. "Can we stop talking about me now? What's *your* family like?"

Callan pursed his lips. "They never came around. I love them, and I know they love me, but I can't be myself around them."

"Well, they're missing out." To his surprise, Cal planted a kiss on his lips, and he couldn't help but laugh. "Hey, I thought we weren't allowed to use sex to avoid our feelings."

"I'm not avoiding my feelings, I'm acting on them." Cal smiled, lips hovering above Shane's. "There's a difference."

His hands slipped underneath the back of Callan's shirt, fingers settling on the man's hips. "I'll take your word for it."

RAISING A FINGER TO HIS LIPS, HE SIGNALED FOR ETHAN TO BE quiet. The hardwood floor threatened to creak underneath his weight. He was surprisingly light on his feet and managed to avoid several spots that normally made noise, except for the last step.

He was standing at a closed closet and could hear giggling behind the door. Opening it quickly, his niece and nephew squealed.

"Gotcha!" He grinned, wrapping an arm around each of them and pulling them into a hug.

"How do you always know where we're hiding?" Harper asked with a giggle.

"I can't tell you that." He clicked his tongue. "It's an Uncle superpower."

Hayden squeezed past him and out of the closet. "So when I become an uncle, you can tell me the secret?"

"Of course!"

"Harper! Hayden!" Nora called from the kitchen.

Shane stepped aside so that the two could go to their mother. He was close behind them but veered into the living room where Ethan sat on the couch.

"Time for bed, you two." Nora hugged and kissed the twins before ushering them into the living room.

"Goodnight, daddy. Goodnight, Uncle Shane!"

Harper and Hayden hugged each of them before going off to their bedrooms. Shane set up one of the gaming systems and then sat on the couch.

Nora kissed her husband's cheek. "I'm going to do some reading."

"Alright, babe. I'll be in shortly." Ethan watched her walk down the hallway.

Shane looked over his shoulder. "Don't I get a kiss?"

Her sigh of frustration could be heard down the hall. "Goodnight, Shane!"

He chuckled and directed his focus to the television.

Ethan raised his brow. "I swear, sometimes I think you love that game more than you love me."

"Well, I *like* the game more than I like you."

Now his brow furrowed. "You don't like me?"

Shane shrugged. "Not all the time."

"Thanks, Shane. That makes me feel much better."

He heaved a sigh, gaze glued to the game on the screen. "People don't always have to like each other to love each other, you know. I mean, can you honestly say that you like *me* all the time?"

"No, I don't. Especially not right now."

"See, point proven. You just don't like the shoe being on the other foot." Swearing under his breath when he lost a round, he set down the controller. "It's normal, man. Don't sweat it."

Ethan rolled his eyes. "Oh, thank you for your insightful philosophies on life, as if you know anything about it."

He turned to face him. "Excuse me?"

"Forget it. Never mind."

"Yeah, I thought not."

"You can't let anything lie, can you?" Ethan got to his feet. "You always have to have the last word."

He threw his hands in the air. "If you're being a prick, I'm not allowed to respond?"

"I'm just giving you a taste of your own medicine."

As Ethan turned down the hall to follow his family to bed, Shane turned off the television. There was no point in staying, he'd clearly pushed his brother to his limit.

TODAY WAS STOCK DAY. THEY HAD TO TAKE INVENTORY AND stock the shelves before the store opened in the afternoon. It was Shane's favorite day because they got to see all the new crystals, and since no two were the same, it always kept his interest.

Peter was humming as he typed at the computer, punching in the names, numbers, and prices while Shane unpacked the boxes.

"Do you have to do that?"

"Is my cheerful disposition bothering you?"

"Yes."

"Good." Peter smirked while Shane rolled his eyes. "Thank you for taking care of me the other night."

He shrugged. "You'd do the same for me."

Peter chuckled, clicking away at the keyboard. "I can't imagine ever seeing you in that condition."

"I'd never let you."

"You know, I don't know whether to be thrilled or

concerned that you haven't made a smartass comment about this yet."

"Why would I?" Shane paused. "But, on a serious note, I don't get paid enough to deal with your emotional trauma, so I'm requesting a raise."

"And there it is." He laughed and shook his head. "Ask and you shall receive."

After placing the last crystal on the counter for Peter to punch in, he threw all the packing material back into the box. "I'm kidding about the raise."

"I'm not."

Shane chewed the inside of his lip. He didn't want Peter to think he'd only helped because he'd expected something in return. But he was always scared to get that deep with someone, and he wasn't willing to go there, so he decided against mentioning it. "Thanks, I guess."

SHANE WASN'T INTO SPORTS, BUT TROY WAS, SO HE DIDN'T mind hanging out and watching a football game. There was food, drinks, and good company, and that was all he needed.

He reached for a fourth slice of pizza and took a bite, speaking with a mouth full. "What are you doing next weekend, Troy?"

"Hanging out with friends."

"You have other friends besides me?"

"Yeah, lots."

"Who would want to be friends with you?" He grinned when Troy shot him a glare. "Do you have to pay them?"

"God, I hope not." Troy shook his head. "I can't afford it."

Since there was a commercial, he muted the TV. "So, how's life? What's new? Still going to that school?"

"Yeah, that's all I've had time for lately."

"Are you going to tell me what you're going to school for?"

He paused, staring at the screen. "No. You won't like it."

Shane furrowed his brow. "Since when do you care what I think?"

"Oh, I care. I just don't let you know it because you'll use it against me."

"That is so rude to assume the worst of me," he said, mockingly rolling his eyes. "I'm going to find out eventually, you know."

"Yeah, I know." Troy turned to him but avoided his gaze. "I'm not ready for things to change yet."

"Ah, come on." Shane nudged him playfully. "How much worse can I get, right?"

"I don't know. Guess we'll find out." Heaving a sigh, he un-muted the TV. "What about you, are you good?"

"Yeah, everything's fine." He shrugged. "There's just...one thing that doesn't make sense to me."

Troy gave him his full attention. "What?"

"That fucking shirt." He burst out laughing, gesturing to the multi-colored disaster. It had strange and abstract shapes that looked as though they were supposed to be animals of some kind. "It's like an ugly fucking Christmas sweater but in t-shirt form."

Troy folded his arms. "It was a gift, okay?"

"Man, how old are you? You need to start dressing yourself."

He shook his head with a chuckle. "Only if you promise to give me some tips."

"Done." Shane finished his slice of pizza, but he was more interested in watching his friend than the game. There was something in his gaze; it reminded Shane of himself, and that was concerning. He'd never seen Troy look troubled before. "Troy?"

"Yeah?"

"You're my best friend."

Troy looked at him, pausing before giving a small nod. "You're mine too."

It was impossible to hide the dark circles under his eyes. Shane was zoning in and out of the conversation and his brother hadn't failed to notice.

"What's wrong, Shane?"

He rubbed his eyes and shook his head. "Nothing."

"Come on, something's bothering you. I can tell."

Taking a deep breath, he looked over the booth they were seated in, and to the TV that hung on the wall. "I don't want to talk about it."

Ethan took a sip of his beer. "I don't understand why you won't talk to me."

"It's not for you to understand. Just leave it alone."

"Okay." He nudged Shane's foot under the table. "Is there anything you *will* talk to me about?"

"I don't know. Pick something and we'll see."

"How's your love life?"

"Everyone wants to know about my love life." Pursing his lips to hide a smile, he moved his gaze from the TV to Ethan. "It's...it's good. Cal's good."

"So, I see." He chuckled. "Do you talk to *him*?"

"No. I mean, we talk. But we avoid a lot of things too."

"By your request or his?"

"Mine. Right now, we're playing this game where we pretend we don't have history." He narrowed his gaze when Ethan raised his brow. "You're judging."

"I'm not, it's just...not a good way to go about a relationship."

"Who said it was a relationship?"

"It isn't?"

Shane shrugged.

"Does he know that?"

"He will."

Ethan shook his head. "You and your secrets."

"Speaking of secrets, have you told Nora?"

"About your heart? No. You asked me not to say anything, and I haven't, but I hope you realize how unfair it is." His gaze was downcast. "I've been with her a long time. It's a little ridiculous that I'm not allowed to say anything. What if mom slips one day and tells her?"

"She won't."

"And what happens if we fail your test of trust?"

He furrowed his brow. "My what?"

"It's a test, isn't it?" Ethan's gaze flicked up to him. "Keeping your secrets and asking us to keep yours. Because Cal hurt you, because mom wasn't there for you like she should have been, because of your heart..."

He shifted uncomfortably. "I guess so."

"Listen, I get needing to protect yourself. But you're going about it in the wrong way," his voice softened. "You have to let people in."

"Yeah, we grew up a bit differently. You learned to trust first, ask questions later." Shane ran his tongue over his front teeth. "I learned to trust that people would hurt me. So, I'd rather keep people at a distance before deciding whether or not I can trust them instead of blindly trusting them and hoping they won't hurt me."

"Jesus, Shane. I didn't realize that mom's lack of acceptance did that much damage." He sighed. "I didn't realize that Callan had hurt you so badly."

"It is what it is."

He paused, gaze wandering over his brother. "You know I love you, right?"

"I know." Shane nodded slowly. "I love you too, man."

7

As small and crappy as the apartment complex was, the community pool was decent. And today, it was empty, which was strange for such a warm day but people probably had better things to do.

Shane yawned and stretched his arms. "Shut up."

Troy furrowed his brow. "I didn't say anything."

"Well, just in case you were thinking about saying something, don't."

Rolling his eyes, he leaned back in the lawn chair. "It's hot."

"And?"

"Don't you want to take your shirt off?"

He shook his head. "No, I'm good."

"Aren't you worried about heat stroke?"

"I'll be alright."

Taking off his sunglasses, Troy raised his brow. "Do you just...not take your shirt off, ever?"

"Nope."

"Not even during sex?"

Shane chuckled. "Nope."

Shaking his head, Troy leaned forward on the table. "What does Callan think about that?"

"He's fine with it. When his options are shirt-on or no sex, he'll take the sex."

Clicking his tongue, he looked toward the pool. "Not even when you shower?"

"Okay, smart-ass. Of course I take it off when I shower."

"Are you really that self-conscious about your body?"

He reached over and patted Troy's stomach. "Well, not all of us were born with six-packs."

"Excuse me?" He scoffed. "I've worked very hard for this body."

"Yeah, that's what I keep telling myself."

"You're a beautiful boy, Shane." He pursed his lips and pet Shane's hair. "Don't you ever doubt it."

"Where have you been all my life?"

He grinned. "At the gym."

Shane laughed and shook his head. "You are something else, Troy."

"I know, and you're lucky to have me. Don't you forget it!"

As the hours ticked by, the air became cooler. He was grateful for that when pulling into the state park for his evening date.

Slinging his bag over his shoulder, Shane walked past the entrance sign and met Callan at their usual spot – the bench where there was a fork in the path.

Cal approached him with a smile. "Anything in there for me?"

"Just a bunch of sarcasm and bad jokes." He grinned and tugged on the strap of his bag. "Oh, you meant this, huh?"

"I'll take your sarcasm and bad jokes any day of the

week." He placed a soft kiss on Shane's lips. "What did you do today?"

"Oh, my usual routine. Got up, got dressed, made someone cry..."

Cal rolled his eyes. "You're not fooling me with that tough guy routine. There's a big softie in there somewhere."

"Only because you haven't made it hard yet."

"Shane Coulter, get your mind out of the gutter!" He playfully smacked his arm. "I'm trying to be serious and you've got jokes."

"Hey, I warned you about that."

As they walked up the path, he reached into his bag and pulled out a package of Pop Rocks. He offered some to Callan, who politely declined, and then sprinkled the contents into his mouth.

Callan laughed. "Why do you still like Pop Rocks? You're supposed to stop eating that shit when you reach puberty."

"How could you not? It's like a party in your mouth."

"If you wanted a party in your mouth, all you had to do was ask."

Shane leaned into him. "Whose mind is in the gutter *now*?"

The dirt path was winding and going on an incline. Shane was used to the exercise but it seemed that Callan was not because his breathing became heavy.

"This is what people who climb Mount Everest must feel like."

"Are you seriously comparing this hill to a mountain?"

"Yes. And when I reach the top, I will die happily because I'm doing this for you."

"Shut up." He clicked his tongue. "We've only been hiking for ten minutes."

Callan heaved a sigh. "Why aren't you as winded as I am?"

"Because I do this all the time."

Shane shoved his hands into his pockets, and when he turned around, realized that Callan was several feet behind him, phone in his hand.

Clicking his tongue, Cal quickly put it away and caught up to him on the path. "Sorry about that. My friend recently rescued a dog from a shelter and she's a little nervous about being a first-time pet owner."

"That's okay, I get it." He smiled softly. "I love dogs."

"You do? Have you ever had one?"

He licked his lips anxiously. It had been a long time since he'd thought about Teddy, let alone spoken about him. "I did, yeah. Once."

"What happened?"

"He ran away."

"I'm sorry." Cal nudged his shoulder. "That must have been hard on you."

"Yeah." He shrugged. "He was only a puppy. But he was my best friend."

"What was his name?"

"Teddy."

Callan pursed his lips. "He didn't have a chip so you could find him?"

"He does, I mean, he did." Shane had never tried to find Teddy, never even entertained the idea. But he couldn't say why. "I guess I just thought he was better off without me."

"I don't see how that could be true. You said he was your best friend. I'm sure you were his too."

Pausing on the dirt path, his hands were balled into fists in his pockets. "I need to take a piss."

Walking on a part of the path that branched off from the

main area, he only stopped when he thought he was out of sight. His hands were shaking, his heart racing as he swung the bag over his shoulder and opened it.

Shane pulled out two bottles of pills and some water, tossing the medication with a gulp of liquid into his mouth. As he swallowed it down, he closed the bag, looked up, and saw Callan staring at him.

Shane's nostrils flared as they watched one another in a sort of stand-off. Rather than explain away the pills, he was intent on staying as far off that subject as possible. In fact, he was so angry that Callan had caught him – as ironic as that was – that he felt the security of their charade these last few months melt away. And everything he'd been holding back came out in six simple words.

"Why the fuck did you leave?"

Callan licked his lips anxiously. "Are we dropping the act?"

"Yes."

He lowered his gaze. "I told you my reason before I left. I couldn't risk alienating my father. I needed his money."

"Yeah, your family's precious reputation was more important than me, I'm aware." Shane threw his hands in the air. "Meanwhile, I was here, all alone, having the worst time of my life because you didn't have the balls to be happy."

"If you want the honest truth, I thought I would get over you." Tears were in his eyes when he met Shane's gaze again. "I thought you would get over *me*."

"And did you?"

"No. Did you?"

"No."

Cal took a step toward him but Shane took a step back.

"I thought it was for the best. You were so young. You needed life experience."

"Don't tell me what I needed. If you want to try and alleviate your guilt, that's fine, but don't use me as an excuse. My age bothered you. Our sexual orientation was a problem for you. It was always about you, Callan."

"You know how people are," his voice was barely above a whisper. "Not everyone is open-minded about age, or sexuality, or-"

"I don't care what people think!"

"*I* do. And you always wanted me to put myself in your shoes but you could never put yourself in mine. If you don't think I struggled these past few years, you're wrong." His bottom lip trembled, tears threatening to spill onto his cheeks. "You looked at me in a way that no one ever has before or since. When you looked at me, I felt loved."

"That's your own fucking fault, Cal. You're the one who left." Turning away, he took a deep breath. "I think it would have been better for me if I had never met you. Then I wouldn't have compared everyone I've ever been with to you, quietly contemplating how they would never measure up. I wouldn't have missed you all this time, I wouldn't have thrown good people away because I kept comparing them to what you and I had. If I had never met you, I wouldn't have wasted my life pining for you, praying that you'd get your shit together and find your way back to me." Swallowing hard, his hand wiped over his face, and he hoped it wasn't obvious that he was swiping tears away. "If I had never met you...then I wouldn't have known what I was missing. And I wouldn't know how lost I am without you." His jaw clenched as he shook his head. "You ruined my life."

"I'm sorry you feel that way because loving you was the best thing that ever happened to me." When Cal stepped forward this time, Shane didn't step away, but he wouldn't look at him either. "You gave me hope in an otherwise dismal world. My life was dark and you brought light into it. No one had ever looked at me the way you did. No one had ever *loved* me the way you did." He took another step forward. "When I went home, I had to pretend that I didn't love you, that I didn't miss you, that I wasn't thinking about you every day. I had to pretend the happiest moments of my life didn't exist and that I didn't know what I had lost. Being with you was like a fantasy, a dream come true that I never wanted to wake from. But I didn't want you to be a fantasy, I wanted you to be my reality." Voice breaking, he closed the distance between them. "I tried so hard to make it work, to find a way to make it real. You were everything I'd ever wished for and everything I thought I would never have. I'm sorry that you regret our relationship because it's the only thing that's kept me going."

Still, Shane refused to look at him. His silence must have been assumed as the end of their relationship, because Callan's shoulders slumped forward in defeat. He turned away, walking back down the path, with Shane watching all the while.

There was a bench not far from the path, settled by a scenic view. With his head in his hands, Shane couldn't see tears, but knew that they were flowing by the way the man's shoulders shook.

It took no time at all to walk to the bench and throw his arms around the blond.

"I'm sorry," he spoke softly. "I didn't realize it was like that for you."

"You never asked. You always just assumed."

"You're right, I did." He wiped away some of Cal's tears

with his sleeve. "I was so focused on what *I* was feeling that I never considered that you might be in pain too."

As he stood up, he kissed the top of Callan's head, lips lingering on his soft hair. "Can I take you to my place?"

"What about my car?"

"I'll drive you back whenever you're ready. I just don't think you should drive when you're upset."

Shane took him by the hand and they started the walk back down the trail.

"You don't have to talk if you don't want to, but if you do, I'm here to listen."

Callan was quiet for a while, the only sound being the crunching of dirt and gravel underneath their shoes. When he did speak, his voice was low and soft. "I have people who love me, I don't doubt that for a second. But they don't know me, not like you do. I can be myself with you and know that you won't judge or criticize me. You're the only person in my life who knows me inside and out and still loves me. You're the only one."

"I'm sorry, Cal. I don't want you to ever feel like I'm not sympathetic about what you've gone through. It's hard for me to see that, despite your troubles, you have a relatively normal life, and that you landed on your feet." He licked his lips anxiously. "I didn't. I've been struggling my whole life, and it changed me. But I do know that my friends and family love and accept me. You didn't have that."

He furrowed his brow, giving Shane's hand a gentle squeeze. "When you tell me these things, it makes me realize that what I've been through isn't that bad."

"No, it is." They came to the entrance and he stopped, turning to face Cal. "Not feeling loved is bad. It's horrible. We're both fucked up in different ways for different reasons, but it doesn't mean that your pain is any less important than mine. It's not a competition. I'm sorry if I've ever made you feel that way."

"You've never made me feel small." He leaned down and kissed the top of Shane's head. "You've always made me feel like I could face anything. You mean everything to me."

He looked away, shaking his head. "Don't give me too much credit. I'm not a good person, Callan."

"You're the most stubborn, moody, unapologetic ass I've ever met." He cupped Shane's chin and tilted it upward so that they were making eye contact. "And you're also the wisest, bravest, most compassionate person I've ever known. I choose you, and I will keep choosing you every day no matter how difficult you make it for me to do so. I love you. Which means I love all those things about you and more."

Shane had to look away to hide the tears in his eyes. "I don't deserve you. I don't deserve anything good."

"Why do you keep saying that? Did someone pound that into your head until you believed it or something?"

"Something like that."

Cal gently touched his arm. "Will you tell me about it someday?"

"Maybe."

The drive to his apartment seemed to take longer than it ever had before. It was silent but he didn't mind because it gave him time to process everything they had discussed.

By the time they walked in the door, Shane was unde-cided about what to do next. He didn't know if they should talk, if he should just listen, or if they should go straight to bed. It hadn't been a long day but the conversation had been exhausting. Unleashing years of feelings could do that to people.

Cal made the decision for him as he headed for Shane's bedroom and climbed into bed. "I missed this place."

"God knows why," Shane mumbled as he followed suit.

"Because this is where you live." He interlocked his fingers on his chest. "This is where we made love for the first time. Do you remember?"

"How the hell could I forget losing my virginity?"

"Well...half of it." Callan grinned. "What was that girlfriend's name?"

"Molly. We never had sex."

Sitting up, he furrowed his brow. "But you said-"

"I lied." He smirked, shifting his gaze to meet Cal's. "I'd done other things, but I'd never had sex with a guy or a girl before."

"Why didn't you tell me?" He clicked his tongue and nudged Shane's arm. "That makes it twice as special."

"It wouldn't have changed anything."

Cal heaved a sigh a laid back down. "Had you been in love before me?"

"I had a boyfriend. And then a girlfriend. I wasn't in love with either of them but I did care for them a great deal." He shifted to his side. "What about you?"

"Before you, I think I was in love...once."

"And after me?"

Callan was quiet for a long period of time. If Shane hadn't been staring at him, he would've thought that he'd fallen asleep. He was wide awake and staring at the ceiling. Just when Shane was about to say that he didn't have to answer, Callan did.

"I fell in love twice while we were apart. I was with a woman for a year and then a man for two years."

"What happened with them?"

"I think I attracted someone my parents would approve of. She seemed like an angel in public. Smart, beautiful, kind. And behind closed doors, she was tearing down my self-esteem, little by little." He pursed his lips. "She belittled me, called me names, made me feel stupid. I even found out that she cheated on me."

"Holy shit. I'm sorry, Cal." Shane placed one hand over Cal's, still interlocked on his chest, and he could feel Callan's racing heart underneath their hands. "What happened with the guy?"

"He was closeted, but he took it a step further. I guess he had a love, hate relationship with me. He said he loved me but treated me as though he hated me." He turned on his side, facing Shane. "It was...a very cold, dark, and lonely place to be in."

"Thank you for trusting me with that. I'm sure it's not easy to talk about."

"Well, you're easy to talk to." Cal chuckled. "I know that's ironic considering you won't open up, but it's true."

"Believe me, I wish I could."

Gaze wandering over Shane, it settled on their hands. "What about the people after me? Can you at least tell me that?"

He shrugged. "I've picked people up at bars. Gone out with some cute guys and pretty girls."

"But you didn't love anyone?"

"No. The minute I first saw you, I knew that you would be it for me. All or nothing. I knew that life would never be the same and that I wouldn't love anyone after you."

Swallowing hard, his eyes filled with tears. "Do you know what I was thinking about when we were apart, when I was with those other people?"

"What?"

"You. And all the ways they couldn't compare." One hand came to Shane's face, thumb gently grazing the sharp cheekbone. "How you would never hurt me. How you loved me more than anyone ever has, more than anyone ever *could*. And better, too."

His bottom lip trembled and he closed his eyes. "Fuck, Cal. Don't make me cry."

"Why not?" he asked softly. "What would be so bad about that?"

"Because if I start, I'll never stop."

Callan pulled Shane closer, chest to chest, and kissed him deeply. Shane's fingers worked their way under Cal's shirt and pulled it upward until it was over his head. Cal tried to do the same to him but he stopped it.

Breathless, Cal broke the kiss and sat up, leaning over him. "But I want to kiss you."

"You *are* kissing me."

"I want to kiss you *everywhere*." He leaned down and nuzzled Shane's neck. "What if I turn off the lights?"

He shook his head. "I'm not ready."

"Okay. I'll stop asking. Except-" He licked his lips. "Can I make love to you, just this once?"

"No. I don't like it."

"So many limitations," he whined before chuckling. "Alright, Shane. I won't cross your boundaries."

"I know. And you're the only one who doesn't complain about the fact that I have them."

"I'm in love with you for you." Callan began a trail of kisses down his neck and then over his shirt. "And I will take you as you are."

DINNER WAS OVER, THE BAR WAS LOUD, AND EVERYONE WAS talking over drinks. Ethan and Troy seemed to be involved in some heavy discussion. Meanwhile, Cal was watching

Shane's brooding expression, and Shane was quite aware of that.

The nightmares had gotten worse. Night after night, Callan had been there to comfort Shane when he awoke.

He wished they could go back home but it was too early to leave. That would have been rude, not that it had ever stopped him before.

"I think everyone deserves a second chance."

Ethan's declaration snapped Shane out of his thoughts.

"Not everyone," he said with a scoff.

"Well, why not? There's a fine line between good and evil. The world is not black and white, there are a lot of gray areas."

Tell that to my nightmares, Shane thought. "Fuck your gray areas, man. You're only saying that because of mom's religious bullshit. Not everyone deserves forgiveness or the chance to redeem themselves. Some people just deserve to rot in Hell." His outburst had silenced the table. He hated that the three of them were staring at him, but it was too late to redirect their attention. "I don't care what anyone says. Bad people can do good things, but it doesn't make up for the bad they've done. They don't deserve *shit*."

Ethan rolled his eyes. "Shane doesn't agree with me, shocking."

"Would you prefer me being a fake person who agreed with you on everything?"

"I'd rather you were a *nice* person."

"Well, this is me, one hundred percent authentic, baby." He took a swig of beer from his glass. "You're just jealous because you don't have the guts to do the same."

Ethan folded his arms. "You think I'm fake?"

"Not completely. But I also don't think you're completely authentic. You act like there's nothing wrong in your life."

"Because I'm happy, you think I'm fake."

"No, I think you're fake because that's not realistic. No one's life is perfect. Just be real, man. It's okay if you have problems for any reason or no reason at all."

"Shane the philosopher." His jaw clenched before he spoke again. "Stop weighing in on my life like you're some kind of expert."

"Upgraded from Shane the Pain to Shane the Philosopher. I'm good with that."

"Oh, you're still a pain."

Troy cleared his throat. "You're awfully quiet, Callan. Aren't you going to state your opinion?"

"I don't know. You both seem pretty set in your beliefs and I don't want to be berated for mine."

That was it. That meant that Cal agreed with Ethan, and Shane couldn't be around people who thought *everyone* deserved forgiveness – that was far too broad a spectrum. Shane was ready to get up from the table, and then Cal took his hand and spoke softly as if he knew that this was a trigger.

"I can't say that everyone deserves to be forgiven, I think it varies from person to person depending on what they've done and who they've harmed. And if they have victims, I would certainly take their stance on the matter into account before daring to form my own opinion."

A lump formed in Shane's throat. Callan knew that something was wrong. Somehow, he knew, whereas Ethan and Troy were oblivious.

"Wow, you must be thrilled." Troy shook his head and laughed. "Someone actually agrees with you, Shane. Congratulations."

"Good." Shane cleared his throat and squeezed Callan's hand. "It's about time I've had someone in my corner."

"Oh, don't be so dramatic, Shane. We're all in your corner. You just won't tell us anything." Ethan emptied his beer bottle. "I'm sure you tell Cal everything."

"Not true. I haven't told him any more than I've said to the rest of you. He just knows me better."

Troy knocked on the table; it was likely his way of easing the tension.. "I'm really happy for you both. I think that's all anyone wants, right? To find our person, the one who's going to understand us and accept us for who we are."

Something on the television caught their attention and Shane was glad for it. While Ethan and Troy were distracted, he leaned against Callan and whispered in his ear, "You weren't just saying that because you thought that's what I wanted to hear, were you?"

"Of course not," he whispered back. "I'll never side with you just to appease you, Shane. But I want you to know that I have your back whether we agree or not."

Shane rested his head on Cal's shoulder. "I sure am glad this is something we agree on."

"What would you have done if it wasn't?"

"I don't know."

"You would have ended this."

Shane pulled back to look at him properly. "What would you have done if I did?"

"I don't know. I'd be lost without you."

"Get a room, you two." Troy had come back with another round of drinks. Shane hadn't even noticed that he'd left the table.

With a smile, Shane's gaze wandered over Callan. "I think we will."

.   .   .

THE DAY WAS ALWAYS MADE BETTER WHEN HE WAS SORTING through a new shipment of stones and Peter was behind the counter, keeping track of the books.

The stereo was on, playing music that wasn't too far off from his normal taste, so he bobbed his head to the beat.

Peter cleared his throat. "How's boy wonder?"

"Who?"

"You know perfectly well who I'm talking about."

He chuckled as he looked toward the counter. "Should we be talking about my personal life at work?"

"Oh, are we not friends anymore?" He mockingly gasped and clutched his chest. "My feelings are hurt."

"We can't have that." Shane clicked his tongue. "I'll be your friend if you beg for my forgiveness."

"Forgiveness?" he scoffed. "I haven't done anything to you, you little shit."

"So that's a no, then?"

"Suck my dick."

Shane grinned and shook his head. "You're not my type, remember?"

"Thank god." He rolled his eyes. "I don't know how Callan puts up with you."

Neither did he. He'd been thinking about that lately, quite a bit. "He'll get sick of me eventually. Everyone does."

"Have you thought about, gee, I don't know, being nice to people?"

"Never crossed my mind." Turning his back to Peter, he continued stocking the empty shelf space. "Being nice never got me anywhere."

He paused, sucking on his teeth. "When were you diagnosed again?"

"I was sixteen."

"So, when did you become such a turd?"

"I don't know. It's not like I flipped a switch, it was a gradual process, I suppose."

"I wasn't always an asshole either."

He stopped to look over his shoulder. "It was your kid, right?"

"Bingo." Peter nodded slowly, his gaze downcast. "When someone you love disappears without a trace...you don't come back from that. People think I'm responsible, did you know that?"

"Yeah, you told me that. You might be an asshole, but you're not a killer."

He lifted his chin. "How do you know?"

"I'd like to think I'm a good judge of character."

"That's questionable. You hang around me, after all." Heaving a sigh, he went between looking at a ledger and clicking keys on the computer keyboard. "Don't you have friends?"

"Yeah, don't you?"

"Yeah. But there's something about you that I like." Peter smiled before tossing a pen at Shane's back. "Can't put my finger on it."

8

Shane kept clenching and releasing his fists. The night-mares were getting worse and his usual ways of coping worked less and less. The only solution that came to mind was not to be better, but to do worse.

Troy was talking about some girl he'd gone out with and Shane was pretending to listen. His eye was on the prize. He nodded several times as though he understood his friend, but they had reached their destination and it had his sole focus.

"Shane, what is this place?"

"We're going to find out."

They stood before a tattered building that had likely been a factory or a warehouse in its heyday. The windows were boarded up and chains were on the doors. There were several signs warning trespassers to keep out. That had never stopped him before.

"Do you trust me?"

"No," Troy scoffed.

"Smart man." He walked up to what he assumed was the back entrance, which seemed to be mostly out of sight except for a few houses in the distance. "You want to get into some trouble?"

"Um...I'd have to think about that."

"Don't think about it too much, your head might explode."

He took out a pin from his pocket and attempted to pick the lock on the back door.

Troy made a sound that he couldn't quite process, something between a pained groaned and a concerned sigh, like the way a parent might sound when their child had gotten into something they shouldn't have. "You can't do that."

"Yes the fuck I can."

"Calm down."

Furrowing his brow, he turned around. "Don't tell me what to do."

He rolled his eyes. "You're a real shit, you know that?"

"I don't know what you mean. I'm a fucking delight."

Turning back to the door, he heard a few clicks. The pin was working.

"Shane, stop it."

"This requires finesse and focus, and you're short on both."

"I mean it." Troy took a step forward, making a scuffing noise on the cement beneath their feet. "If you go through with this, I'm calling the cops."

Removing the pin from the lock, he turned to face him once more. "Are you fuckin' serious?"

"I have to, Shane." His voice was quiet, almost mousy, which was very unlike him.

"Why?" Shane threw his hands in the air. "Because you're so morally righteous?"

"Because I'm fresh out of the academy and you'd be breaking the law."

He gasped as if someone had punched him in the chest. It didn't seem real. How could his best friend be a cop and he knew nothing about it?

Thinking back on any time they'd spent together recently, it had been building to this. Troy had made comments – Shane had picked up on the hints – but he couldn't have imagined that this would be the outcome.

"Fuck you." Swallowing hard, he shook his head. "You're lying."

Troy clenched his jaw, his gaze unfaltering. "I'm not lying. I'm an officer of the Westbourne, Michigan police department."

Shane had to rub his chest because it suddenly felt very tight. "Why the fuck would you do that to me?"

"Because it's not all about you, Shane!" Heaving a sigh, Troy smoothed both hands over his face before letting them fall to his sides. "This is *my* life and I don't need your approval to live it the way I want to."

That was true. It didn't mean that it didn't sting. Shane had never thought that Troy would do something to end their friendship. If anything, Shane had thought that he would be the one to push Troy too far. That was an outcome he'd always been prepared for. This was not. "You know how I feel about cops. I can't be friends with a cop."

"That's fine." Troy's nostrils flared and there were tears in his eyes. "You weren't a very good friend anyway."

The boiling in his blood was unlike anything he'd ever felt before, and he didn't like it. His hands were balled into fists, his breathing heavy with the effort of not throwing a punch.

This was a line he'd been struggling not to cross for years. Once there was physical violence in a relationship, there was no going back.

But this was a betrayal. Troy had done something unforgivable and he was just trying to catch up. Not willing to give himself time to calm down or reconsider what he was about to do, Shane's fist collided with his friend's face with such force that it knocked him down.

The look of shock on his face made Shane's cheeks flush red, instantly feeling deep shame. Yet, his anger would not subside, and it only fueled Troy's.

Shane was knocked to the ground and the two of them rolled around, trying to get the upper hand. Both landed punches and he could feel his skin splitting, first on his eyebrow and then his lip. It was only when blood poured from his nose that he held up his hands.

"Truce!"

Breath heavy, arm still held back to hit Shane again, Troy's gaze wandered over his face. "Why are you bleeding so much?"

"I'm on blood thinners," he answered breathlessly.

"What the fuck?" Quickly getting to his feet, he held out his hand to help Shane up. "Why would you start a fight when you're on blood thinners? Do you have a goddamn death wish?"

"Wouldn't you like to know?" Swatting Troy away, he stood up but immediately doubled over, pressing a sleeve to his nose. "We've got to...we need to go."

"Fuck, come on."

Forcing Shane's arm around his neck for support, Troy helped him into the back seat of his car. He put the key into the ignition and drove off as fast as he could.

"I'm getting blood everywhere," Shane mumbled.

"I don't care, you idiot! Just don't die, alright?"

"Depends on how fast you drive."

He tried to stay awake as his eyes rolled back. His limbs

were getting heavier by the minute. There were voices around him – more than just Troy's now, but everything was a blur and he couldn't make out the questions they were asking him, let alone answer them.

When his eyes opened again, he was in a bed with two IVs in his arm. He scrunched his nose, the taste of copper still fresh on his tongue.

Looking down, he noticed that he'd been changed out of his clothes and into a hospital gown. His nostrils flared, fists clenched as it occurred to him that Troy might have seen the marks on his skin, the ones he'd been hiding for years.

When his former best-friend pulled back the curtain and stood by his bedside, he looked almost as bad as Shane felt – eyes red and puffy, skin eerily pale.

"Shit, if I didn't know any better, I'd say *you'd* been the one bleeding out."

Troy rolled his eyes. "Glad to see you didn't lose your sense of humor."

"That's in my head, not my veins."

Silence fell between them. Shane's gaze didn't waver, but Troy's did.

"I'm not pressing charges, Shane."

"I guess that makes you a saint."

He shook his head. "You don't get a pass for being an asshole just because you almost died."

"And you don't get a pass for being one just because you're a cop."

With a scoff, Troy folded his arms. "Friends don't keep secrets, Shane."

"Then I guess it's a good thing we're not friends anymore."

He opened his mouth and then closed it. His jaw was

clenched for what seemed like half an hour before he spoke. "Have a nice life."

Another slide of the curtain and Troy was gone. He swallowed hard, allowing that to sink in. Shane hadn't wanted their friendship to end. This wasn't how he'd wanted Troy to find out that he was unhealthy. If he really thought about it, he could convince himself that it was better this way. One less person he had to keep secrets from.

He had half a mind to rip out the IVs and go home, but he could hardly move and his body wouldn't stop shaking.

"Mister Coulter," came the disapproving voice of a doctor. "Back again, I see."

Shane heaved a sigh, mostly because he was annoyed with the man's tone. "Oh, don't act like you're not happy to see your favorite masochist."

"You're lucky your friend got you here so quickly. I don't know what possessed you to pick a fight in your condition."

"How do you know I started it?"

"You said so yourself. You're a masochist."

"Don't act like you know anything about me, doc. All you know is what's on your fuckin' chart."

Making a few notes on the clipboard, he stepped closer to the curtain. "As long as you're feeling better tomorrow, you'll be discharged in the morning."

"Great. Thanks."

He knew that he wouldn't be getting much sleep, not with the nurses who would be coming in and out, making sure he was still alive. As soon as the doctor left, Shane closed his eyes, his body still shaking under the blanket. All he wanted to do was rest. But he hadn't been able to do that in years.

Hearing the curtain pull back again, he opened his

mouth to give the doctor an earful, except it wasn't who he'd been expecting.

"Cal?"

"Jesus, Shane." Leaning over the bed, he gently kissed his forehead. "You look like death warmed over."

"Wow, thanks for sugarcoating it."

"What the hell happened?"

"Is it okay if I don't want to talk about it?"

Pulling back, Callan gave him a stern look. "From what I heard, you're lucky to be alive."

"Who told you that?"

"Troy did. He's the one who called me."

"Mmm." Sighing softly, he nuzzled Cal's nose. "I'm glad you're here."

"I'm not going anywhere."

"I don't know about that. I might scare you off."

"Never." Callan kissed him softly. "Can I get you anything?"

"I'm fine."

Looking back at the chair beside the bed, and then back at Shane – who was shivering – he pursed his lips. "Do you think there's room for me in the bed? That chair looks really uncomfortable."

Shane stared at him for a moment. Callan must have known that he wasn't going to ask for help even if he needed it, but the extra body heat would make him feel a little better. "I think I can make room."

After he moved over, Cal kicked off his shoes and climbed into the bed, carefully curling his body against Shane's as if he might break him. "Am I hurting you?"

"No." Pressing his back against Callan's chest, he took a deep breath. The shaking lessened within minutes. And while he'd never admit it, the man's presence was incredibly comforting. He needed that more than he could ever say. "Th-thank you."

Smiling softly, he kissed the back of Shane's neck. "I love you too."

HOLDING HIM A LITTLE TIGHTER, CAL'S NOSE GRAZED THE TOP of Shane's spine. He hadn't gotten much sleep, too concerned about his lover's body language. Shaking, groaning, whimpering – and Cal had tried to soothe the sleeping man through it all.

The curly-haired brunette shifted toward him, cheeks wet with tears. Cal pressed a kiss to his forehead before wiping Shane's cheek with his thumb, prompting him to open his eyes.

"What are you doing?" he asked in a groggy voice.

"You were crying in your sleep."

"Must be whatever they gave me."

Cal wiped the remainder of Shane's tears with his sleeve. "Are you sure you're okay?"

"Just tired."

"I know. You didn't even stir when the nurses came in."

"Did they say I could leave?"

"Yeah, if you feel up to it."

Having woken up free of IVs, Shane climbed out of bed.

Clicking his tongue, Cal sat up. "Shane, please be careful, if you start to bleed again-"

"I'm fine, I'm fine." He leaned back to pat Callan's leg. "If I wasn't okay, I wouldn't be able to move."

Knowing that nothing he said would be taken to heart, he sighed in defeat. "At least let me help you get dressed."

"Nope."

Cal begrudgingly handed Shane his blood-stained

clothing and watched him disappear into the bathroom. He approached the door, listening for sounds of a stumble or fall.

"It's really unsanitary to put those back on, you know."

"Whatever," came his muffled reply. "Almost done."

"Why won't you let me see you?"

"Because it's ugly."

"What, your body?"

"Yes."

His breath hitched in his throat, hand gently pressed against the door as if Shane could feel him. "That's not true. Every part I've seen is beautiful."

He opened the door, shaking his head. "Trust me, it isn't."

"What is it that you're hiding then? A birthmark?"

"Scars." His gaze fell, jaw clenched. "Lots of them."

Furrowing his brow, Cal gently rubbed Shane's arm. "Are they self-inflicted?"

"Yes. They're bad." He pinched the bridge of his nose, cheeks flushing red. "Really bad."

"Come here." Cal pulled him into a gentle embrace. It pained him to think that Shane was concerned about his reaction to such a thing. He'd failed to make the man he loved feel safe, and there was no worse feeling than that. "You have nothing to be ashamed of. But you don't have to show me if you don't want to."

"I'm just not...I don't..." He took a deep breath. "I'm fucked up. I don't deserve good things."

"That couldn't be further from the truth. Is that why you won't let me make love to you, because you don't think you deserve it?"

"That's one of the reasons."

"But wouldn't that feel better than what we normally do?

What if your skin breaks somehow and you start bleeding, and-"

"It hasn't, and it won't. We've been careful."

Callan pulled back to gaze at him. "I've seen some of the bruises that you've had as a result. You try to keep your skin covered, but I see them sometimes." Eyes filling with tears, his voice broke when he said, "I don't like knowing that I've done that to you."

"You're not hurting me, Cal. I like it rough, okay? I just bruise easily." Shane placed his hands on Callan's chest. "If you were really hurting me, you'd know. I would tell you."

"I just want to be soft, and gentle, and loving with you." He shook his head. "Why won't you let me? Help me understand."

Rolling his eyes, Shane returned to the side of the bed, gathering his belongings. "I already told you, it's over-stim-ulation."

His tone was an indication that Callan was pushing the boundary. It was something he'd struggled with since their reunion, but there was only so much he could ignore. "Is it because of how you've hurt yourself in the past?"

"Yeah, I guess." Heaving a sigh, he set the hospital bag on the bed. "Look, I don't really know. It is what it is."

Pursing his lips, Cal folded his arms. "Why do you hate being comfortable?"

"Because if I'm comfortable, bad things could happen."

He paused, gaze wandering over the blood-stained clothing on his boyfriend. It seemed like an odd sentiment to have without knowing where it had come from. With so many secrets between them, it seemed like they were oceans apart. "You don't know that."

Shane shot him a look. "Neither do you."

· · ·

WHEN HE OPENED THE DOOR, HE FURROWED HIS BROW, HAVING expected a much larger crowd. Instead, it was just Ethan.

"Where's Nora and the kids?"

"I didn't want to overwhelm you."

"Overwhelm me?" Shane closed the door, then narrowed his gaze while facing his brother. "Who told you, hmm? Was it Callan?"

"No, it was Troy."

Rolling his eyes, he folded his arms. "Figures. But, as you can see, I'm fine."

"I wouldn't go that far."

"Are you saying I look like shit or something?"

Ethan swallowed hard. "I think we should talk."

"Uh-oh. Are you breaking up with me?"

"Man, I'm being serious."

"Okay." Raising his hands defensively, he walked to the couch and gestured for Ethan to sit down. "What do you want to talk about?"

"You have to cool it with the attitude. Sometimes it's funny, but you're at an age when you need to start growing up. You shouldn't talk to people the way you do."

Oh, so it was going to be *that* kind of talk. "I'm an adult. I can do and say whatever I want and I don't have to answer to you."

He threw his hands in the air. "This is what I mean. You're walking around with this teenage angst, except you're not a teenager anymore, Shane. You're so goddamn moody all the time. No matter what I say, there's a smartass reply soon to follow."

"I'm not going to change for you. Or for anyone." He scoffed and shook his head. "I love my niece and nephew, and they're the only people who will be spared from my snark. They're children. They're innocent." Shane paused, lowering his gaze. "They don't deserve to be treated like that."

"Oh, but *I* do?"

"You can handle it."

Ethan wore an incredulous expression. "It's ridiculous that you somehow think that makes it okay. You can't justify your shitty behavior that way."

He shrugged, gaze lifting to his brother, who was still standing. "Sure I can."

"Look, my kids are getting older. Nora's seen and heard enough that it makes her...cautious." Heaving a sigh, he took a step toward the couch. "She doesn't want any bad influences around our kids and neither do I."

"I already told you that I'm perfectly capable of controlling myself around my niece and nephew."

"You can see how that might be difficult for us to believe."

"So what are you saying?" He furrowed his brow. "That if I don't knock it off, you won't let me see the kids anymore?"

"We don't want to do that." Ethan's voice softened. "But we do want our kids to have good role models."

Shane swallowed hard, his nostrils flaring. "Why the fuck did you come back here then?"

"We didn't come back to be subjected to your bullshit, I can tell you that."

"My bullshit. That you left me to stew in for five years."

"Is that why you're acting this way? Revenge?" Ethan sighed exasperatedly. "Adults talk through these things; they don't treat each other like crap out of spite."

"This isn't spite, this is who I am. And just because you don't like it doesn't mean it's wrong." Getting up from the couch, Shane walked right past his brother and opened the apartment door. "I like who I am, it's not my problem if you don't."

Ethan stared at him for a moment. Shane stared back, but his gaze was much harder. Eventually, the elder brother's jaw clenched, and he walked out, leaving the younger one to hide his tears behind the closed door.

SHANE UNLOADED ONE BOX OF CRYSTALS AFTER ANOTHER, GAZE flicking to Peter behind the desk every few minutes. He looked worse than Shane felt, like he was coming off a bender. Once or twice, Shane had seen him in such a state before and typically ignored it – Peter was an adult and he could handle it. But today, he couldn't ignore it.

"You don't look so good."

Peter raised his brow. "Neither do you."

"Whatever." Taking a deep breath, he went back to unpacking the boxes.

"I'm serious. You're more pale than usual. Moodier too, if that's even possible."

"What do you care?"

"Hey." Walking out from the desk, he approached Shane. "I care."

Gaze wandering over him, he shook his head. He didn't like that the subject of conversation had turned to him, so he attempted to avoid it by moving on to the next shelf. "What's your deal?"

"My *deal*?"

"Don't make fun of the way I speak, I'm not in the mood." Licking his lips, he looked over the shelf to make eye contact with his boss. "You own a business you don't care about, you have the reputation of a twenty year old playboy, and all of this sudden, you give a shit about me."

"I've never *not* given a shit."

"Fine. But you don't get to do this anymore."

"Do what?"

"Go back and forth between being professional and personal."

"Isn't that what *you* do, Shane?" He walked around the shelf so that there were no obstacles between them. "You set boundaries. Everyone has to play by your rules. Guess it's not fun to be on the receiving end, is it?"

"Uh-uh. No. You don't get to harp on me for my fuckin' attitude and then act like it's okay to treat me the same way." Scrunching his nose, he spoke through gritted teeth. "I can't stand hypocrites."

Peter's gaze fell to the carpeted floor. "You're right and I'm sorry. You're very comfortable being who you are and I shouldn't try to change that. You have your reasons and so do I." He returned to his place behind the desk.

Heaving a sigh, Shane approached, leaning against the counter. "You, uh...want to talk about it?"

"I lost the only person who was in my corner. Lost my job, my wife, and everything in between. So I started over and became the complete opposite of who I was before." Clicking away on the keyboard, he shrugged. "People still talk shit about me, but my new-found attitude makes me care less."

"If we're so alike, why do you give me so much shit?"

He paused. "Because I don't want you to be like me, kid. I'm lonely. I pretend not to care when I do, which sends very mixed messages to anyone who tries to get close to me." Peter swallowed hard, stepping away from the computer. "I'm not happy. Can you say that you are?"

"I'm taking a personal day, I'm too tired to deal with this shit." With a wave of his hand, Shane turned on his heel.

"I'm sorry, kid. You got a bad deal. But being sick isn't an excuse to be an asshole."

"But losing your kid is?" He stopped in his tracks, regretting the words as soon as they'd left his mouth.

"Touché."

Turning back around, he was just in time to see the tears in Peter's eyes. "Pete, I'm sorry. I didn't mean-"

"Yeah, you did. And it's okay, you're right." He cleared his throat before disappearing into the back room.

Shane closed his eyes, hand slamming down on the counter. He was really on a roll this week, wasn't he? "Fuck."

9

His fingers tapped the counter-top anxiously. It had been hours since he'd heard from Callan. Licking his lips, he read over the text again.

I have a surprise for you.

Shane hated surprises, and Cal knew that. Of course, he had asked what it was and his boyfriend had left him on read.

So, when there was finally a knock on the door, he sprinted toward it and yanked it open.

"Surprise!"

Shane's gaze fell from Callan's beaming face to an aged German Shepard at his feet. The dog was panting, head tilted.

"You brought me a dog?" he asked with a chuckle. "An *old* dog?"

"Well, this isn't just any old dog." Cal lifted his chin proudly. "This is *your* old dog."

Shane opened his mouth and closed it again. It took a moment for the words to register in his brain. "What do you..." He trailed off, knowing exactly what he'd meant, because Shane had only ever had one pet. "It can't be him." Shaking his head, he placed his hands on his hips. "It's not-I mean, there's no way."

"Well, it is! I know he's older now, but I think he still has a few good years left in him." Cal leaned down to ruffle the fur on the dog's head. "Isn't that right, buddy? His owners surrendered him because of, well, his age. That's more common than I wanted to believe, apparently."

The German Shepard barked, and when he did, his ears stood up. And there it was, the confirmation that it was, indeed, his childhood pet. One ear looked as though the tip had been cut off.

"T-Teddy?" his voice broke.

The dog barked eagerly, as if, at that very moment, he recognized Shane too.

Falling to his knees, he reached out a shaking hand to touch the animal's fur. It was coarser than he remembered, but still soft. There was gray in his coat. But those eyes – those aged, soulful eyes, had seen things that no one else had. Teddy and Shane shared a unique bond, one he didn't have with anyone else in his life, still to this day.

Teddy knew the truth.

Wrapping his arms around him, Shane buried his face in Teddy's fur.

"Jesus, Shane, are you alright?" Callan bent down, pressing a hand to his back. "You really missed him, didn't you?"

"You d-don't understand," he said through tears. "I thought he was dead."

"Hey, come on, let's get you both inside." Cal helped Shane to his feet and gently tugged Teddy's leash, walking them both inside before closing the door.

He guided them to the couch, Shane sitting down and

Teddy jumping up to curl on his lap, sending Shane into another fit of tears.

"Oh, babe..." Cal sat down beside them, stroking Shane's curls. "I had no idea he meant so much to you. I knew it was a long shot, but I wanted to do something nice for you. So I started asking around, going from shelter to shelter, looking online, got the chip information from your mom-"

"You went to my mom?"

"Yes." He paused. "I hope that's okay."

"Yeah, I just-" Shane sniffled and wiped his eyes. "I can't believe she still had the information."

"She wanted to see you smile just as much as I did. But I made you cry instead."

He took in a gasping breath. "I'm sorry, I don't know why I'm so emotional."

"I've never seen you like this. Not even...before I left." Cal moved as close as possible with the dog lying on the couch, and wrapped his arm around Shane's shoulders. "I think I know why. Your mother called to check on my progress. And she told me what happened between you and Ethan."

"I can't be what he wants me to be." Sniffling again, he shook his head. "He wants me to let my guard down *all* the time, and I can't. Tomorrow, I have to pretend like this meltdown never happened. That's how I function."

"I know, it's okay." He kissed the top of Shane's head. "We won't speak of it after tonight. Let's order pizza and binge-watch something with Teddy."

"Okay." Shane nodded. "God, I forgot to ask. Is that even his name?"

"I don't think it matters. He remembers the name you gave him."

· · ·

He closed the curtains, allowing the artificial light to take over the natural in the apartment. It was a very special night and Shane wanted to make sure that everything was at its best, including him. He took a shower, put on his nicest shirt, and even wore a necklace and bracelet, both bought from the stone and gem shop.

It wasn't as though he never put effort into his looks, or the time they spent together, but tonight was different. Even Teddy seemed excited. He was sitting by the door, waiting patiently for their guest.

"Hey, buddy. We have a lot to talk about, huh?"

Teddy sat up, wagging his tail. Shane reached for the shelf next to the door and grabbed a chew toy. It was a stuffed hamburger with a squeaker inside. He gave it a squeeze before tossing it to Teddy, who caught it mid-air.

With a smile, he knelt down, playing a gentle tug-of-war with the old dog.

"I don't even know where to begin except to say...that I'm sorry." Swallowing hard, he sat on the floor, hand combing through Teddy's fur. "I was trying to protect you. You know that, right? That's all I do, try to protect everyone. But they don't know that's what I'm doing. And I can never tell them."

Teddy laid down, though he kept his head up as if listening to every word.

"The only reason I can talk to you about it is because you already know, don't you?" Raising a shaking hand, his fingers carefully moved over the ear that was missing its tip. "I don't know if you remember what happened, but I do. I remember everything. And I'll never forgive myself for it."

Teddy whined and rested his head on his paws.

"I've thought about you every day. I can't believe you even remember me, Teddy. And I really can't believe that Callan found you. I shouldn't be surprised though, he's been very good to me since he came back. And I've been...well, frankly, a shit." His gaze was downcast as he shook his head. "I shouldn't be with him. It's not safe. I just can't bring myself to let him go."

Meeting the gaze of his childhood pet, Shane stroked his back. "You shouldn't be here either, you know. But you've been abandoned twice now. That's not going to happen again. I just don't know who's going to take care of you if you outlive me. I've pushed everyone away." He placed a kiss on the dog's head. "That's why I'm doing this for Callan. I want him to know how much he means to me, even if I can't come right out and say it."

A knock at the door ignited a bark from the old dog. Shane chuckled and stood up to open the door.

"I'm chopped liver now that you're here."

"Oh, I'm sure that's not true." Callan greeted him with a kiss before stepping inside. "You two have history."

"Yeah, but *you* saved his life." Kicking the door shut, he realized that he had done that too. Not that Teddy would understand. At least in Cal's instance, Teddy had been whisked away from a place of boredom and loneliness. For all *he* knew, Teddy might resent him. "He might end up becoming your dog after all of this."

Clicking his tongue, he set a bottle of wine on the counter. "Why would you say that?"

"I was different the last time he saw me. I wasn't, you know...Shane the Pain."

"If he's anything like me, he'll love you to death just as you are."

His cheeks flushed pink and he cleared his throat. "Quit it with the compliments, will you? I don't want to get all mushy. Not even today."

Placing his hands on Shane's hips, Cal tugged him

forward to close the distance between their bodies. "Are you my present?"

He tilted his head back and forth as if he was thinking. "Partially."

"Oh, there's more?" Leaning in, he placed a kiss on Shane's neck. "More than this?"

"Just a little." One hand tucked underneath Cal's chin, the other squeezed his ass. "Can you wait?"

"For you? Forever."

Rolling his eyes, he gave Cal's ass a smack before they walked to the kitchen.

Dinner was eaten at the table, consisting of three courses, all being favorites of Callan's; Caesar salad, homemade spaghetti, and chocolate mousse for dessert.

While he was finishing the mousse, Shane pursed his lips, gaze moving to Teddy, who was begging for scraps, and Cal, who was scrolling through something on his phone.

Catching the reproachful look, the blond set his phone on the table. "I'm sorry, it's work."

"Normally, I'd tell you off. But since it's your birthday..."

He smiled and pushed his phone away. "Would you mind if we talked shop?"

"Not if you want to." The smile on Callan's face grew. It was contagious. "Come on, spill. You're clearly excited about something."

"Well, it feels wrong to be excited considering the subject, but I am pleased to be working on such an important piece."

A piece. He was talking about journalism. "Are you going to make me guess?"

"I'm writing an article about a series of strange events; missing people, mysterious disappearances, and a string of murders that I believe are the work of one person." He paused. "Or, rather, one person with a lot of assistance."

Shane nodded slowly. "So, you didn't give up on journalism."

"Nope." He grinned. "Are you proud of me?"

"Very." Not that his tone gave way to that. "What makes you think it's the work of one person?"

"Well, it's the oddest thing. Although none of the crimes appear to be connected, the victims are all of a similar personality. They were kind, compassionate, some even heroic, actively helping others. You know when you see those documentaries, and people say that the victim or perpetrator were really nice, but then the truth comes out that not everything was as it appeared to be? In this case, it's accurate. Not a single person has anything bad to say about them. They were happy, healthy, and everyone loved them. It-" He paused, seemingly to collect his thoughts. "It's almost as though someone's harming people who are trying to make a difference."

"Hmm." While Callan was clearly enthusiastic about this project, Shane couldn't bring himself to feign excitement, not even on Cal's behalf. "Interesting."

He heaved a sigh. "You think it's far-fetched?"

"I don't know." Shane folded his arms. "I'm into fiction, I don't have an investigative eye like you do."

"But you're a writer. I respect your opinion, personally and professionally."

"I was never professional. I haven't even written a word in years." Trying to wipe the look of discomfort from his face, he leaned on the table. "If this makes you happy, then I'm happy *for* you. How about that?"

"I'll take it." He flipped his phone face-down before slipping his hand over Shane's. "I might not go with that article.

I have other ideas. That's just the bigger story, the one people might really care about, you know?"

"I care about *you*."

"Is that your way of changing the subject?"

He smirked. "Maybe."

"Does the subject matter bother you?"

"I don't know." He waved his free hand in the air. "It'd be disturbing if it was true."

"It's something I can relate to, I suppose. The threat of death. Not that I'm trying to make a difference."

"Well, aren't you?"

He chuckled. "I guess so." Cal's thumb moved back and forth over Shane's knuckles. "My grandfather threatened to kill me over my sexuality."

"He did?" Jaw clenched, he tried to ease the growing tension in his hand, not wanting to inadvertently hurt Cal's fingers. "Let me at 'im, I can take him."

Cal laughed and shook his head. "You and what army?"

"Just me."

"I imagine the army of Shane is the best of them all." He brought Shane's hand to his lips. "I know you would fight for me fiercely with everything you have."

Giving his hand a gentle squeeze, Shane got to his feet. "Come on. I know you said no presents, but I have a surprise for you."

He took Callan by the hand, pulling him into the bedroom. It was decorated with multiple displays full of red roses, Cal's favorite. There were petals on the bed and candles lit on both the bedside table and the dresser.

Callan bent over to pick up the card that was placed in the middle of the bed. Inside was a hand-written poem that read:

In your arms, I feel blessed
Your hearts is as deep as the sea
No words could ever express
How much you mean to me

With tears in his eyes, he turned to face Shane. "You said that you haven't written a word in years."

"I haven't." Shane placed his arms around Cal's waist. "But I wanted to do something special for you. I know it's shit, but-"

"No, it isn't. I love it. I can't believe you did all of this for me."

"It's your birthday. What kind of a person do you think I am?"

He pressed his hand to the small of Shane's back. "Thank you. I mean it. I know that you can't say how you feel about me, but you're showing it."

A twinge of guilt settled in his chest. Swallowing hard, he started unbuttoning Cal's shirt. "You do know how I feel, don't you?"

"Yes, love." He smiled softly. "I do."

His fingers worked quickly to remove the shirt, though his own remained in place – as usual, and then jeans, and underwear followed soon after before they fell back on the bed. Shane was on top, pushing away some of the rose petals from between Cal's legs.

One kiss was delivered to the birthday man's stomach, causing a sharp intake of breath. Shane smiled and trailed soft kisses up his chest, along his neck, and stopped at his lips.

"There he is." Cal brushed back curls from Shane's forehead. "There's the Shane I know. Tender and loving."

Clenching his jaw, he averted his gaze. "The Shane you knew died when you left."

He cupped Shane's cheeks in his hands, gently turning his face so that he could look him in the eyes. "I'm never going to leave you again."

Taking a deep breath, Shane blinked back tears. "I'm only going to offer this once because I know how much it means to you. What if..." Even though he was the one making the offer, the words were still difficult to get out. "What if *I* make love to *you*?"

"Are you sure?" He furrowed his brow. "I don't want to overstimulate you. If you're uncomfortable, I won't enjoy it."

"I think I'll be alright if I'm the one taking control. I want to be sweet to you, I just can't let you be so gentle with *me*."

"I understand." Cal searched Shane's gaze – a typical trait of his, especially when he was looking for any sign of hesitation. "And I accept your generous offer."

He rolled his eyes. "Don't make it sound like some transaction. I want to make love to you, for God's sake."

"No, not for His sake. For mine." Cal pursed his lips in an effort to contain his emotions, but it didn't work, a tear escaped from his eyelid, which Shane promptly wiped away. "Thank you, Shane."

With Teddy at the foot of the bed, Callan was careful not to kick him as he pulled his lover in closer. His nose nuzzled the back of Shane's neck. A hand reached to tug down the white t-shirt, respecting the younger man's privacy, despite how easy it would have been to sneak a peek.

"Morning," he mumbled, tiredness evident in his graveled voice.

Shane moaned in response and Cal chuckled.

"Come on, sleepyhead. You were so good to me last night. I want to return the favor, but in the way that *you* like this time."

Another moan, and then it turned into a whimper. Furrowing his brow, Cal cupped Shane's shoulder and gave it a gentle shake.

"Baby, wake up."

More whimpers were accompanied by gasps and Cal's attempts to wake him grew desperate, shaking him with more force before rolling him flat on his back.

Shane's eyes sprung open and Cal placed a hand on his heaving chest. "It's alright, I'm here. I'm here."

His gaze traveled down the disheveled t-shirt, lingering on the part of his abdomen that had been revealed.

"Shane, what-"

"Get the fuck off me."

The dainty brunette rolled to the edge of the bed, feet pressing firmly to the floor.

Blinking rapidly, he tried to erase what he'd just seen from his mind, but how could he? Jagged marks near his navel that looked as though they had been carved with a knife, flesh raised and ghostly white from the scarring.

Mouth ajar, he waited for Shane to get to his feet before addressing it. "What the fuck did I just see?"

"Something you shouldn't have. I fucking told you not to look at me."

"You were having a nightmare, Shane. I was trying to help you, I didn't mean to invade your privacy." With Shane's back still facing him, he swallowed hard. "You...did that to yourself?"

"Yes," he grumbled.

"Does your family know about this?"

"Some of them." He turned to face Callan, jaw clenched.

"I knew I could get away with it at my dad's house, so that's what I did during the summer. They usually healed by the time I went back to my mom's."

"I don't understand." He scooted to the edge of the mattress, feet on the floor and hands on the waistband of Shane's boxers. "The doctors, nurses, and your father, they...they saw what you did to yourself and they never tried to help you?"

"No," he answered with a scoff. "You don't know how people look at me. Because I was self-destructive, they judged me and ignored my cries for help. People don't want to deal with it. I cut myself, got into fights deliberately, and people don't care about things they don't understand."

"You wanted help and no one gave it to you?" His bottom lip trembled. "I would have. You know that, don't you?"

"I know." Shane avoided his gaze but placed his slender fingers over Cal's. "This was all over by the time I met you."

"I should have asked you back then. Maybe things would have turned out differently."

"They wouldn't have. I was still too young for you, remember?"

Heaving a sigh, he stood up, towering over Shane. "I'm trying to be better. I'm trying to understand you. And I can't do that if you won't let me in. What drove you to harm yourself like that?"

"Being attracted to men wasn't accepted in my family either. Not at the time, anyway."

Chewing his bottom lip anxiously, he chose his next words carefully. "Shane, did someone help you with those cuts?"

He furrowed his brow, gaze still avoiding Cal's. "Why would you ask me that?"

"Because, well, this story I'm looking into, I've

seen...some things. I've studied and done my research, and those scars – they're at such an angle, I don't think you could have done them on your own."

"I did them myself."

"Hey, you can tell me. Whoever it was, if it was a friend or something, I'm not looking to get them in trouble. I just want to know what happened."

"If you don't fucking believe me then you can get out."

"That's not what I meant."

"Yes, it is. You're calling me a liar."

"Shane, that's not-"

"Get the fuck out of my face."

Stepping away from the bed, he whistled for Teddy to follow him out of the room and into the kitchen. Teddy obliged.

Slipping on his shirt and jeans, Cal stood at the counter, waiting for Shane to acknowledge him. Instead, the raven-haired man tended to Teddy, filling his water bowl and giving him a scoop of kibble.

Eyes brimming with tears, Cal approached him slowly. "Don't do this. Please don't push me away."

"Out." He waved a hand in the air, gesturing toward the door.

Knowing that it wouldn't be wise to overstay his welcome, Callan gathered his things, even refraining from a kiss before exiting the apartment.

NOW THAT HE HAD SUCCESSFULLY ALIENATED EVERYONE IN HIS life, Shane dined alone. He wished that Teddy could come along as his emotional support dog, but he was worried about being seen with anyone – human or animal – that he cared about.

Looking over the menu at the restaurant, he tried to find something that sounded good. Nothing did. He didn't want to eat. At this point, he was simply going through the motions.

"Shane?"

Placing the menu on the table, he looked up to see a middle-aged woman with long, dirty-blonde hair and dull blue eyes. "Uh-" He felt as though he'd been caught in some sort of trap, even though he'd done nothing wrong, and she had never made him feel uncomfortable. "Missus Talbot, it's good to see you. I mean, not good, but-"

"Relax, honey," she said with a warm smile. "It's good to see you too."

He gestured to the empty chair across his table. "Please, have a seat."

"I was on my way out, I just happened to see you and...well, I couldn't pretend I didn't. It's been a long time since I've seen you face to face."

If she wasn't going to sit, Shane felt obligated to stand up. Showing her that small gesture of respect was the least he could do.

Looking her in the eye seemed impossible, but if he didn't, that would send the wrong message. He wanted her to know how much he liked her. And how much guilt he carried; not that it would make her feel any better or bring her son back. "I'm sorry. I always mean to call but I never know what to say."

"It's okay." She gave him a teary smile. "I still get your cards every year. I keep all of them."

He swallowed hard. "I think about him all the time."

"I'm glad to hear that. I don't want him to be forgotten." Head bowed, her voice broke as she uttered her next words. "Sometimes I can't remember what he sounded like, you know? Just his voice, the jokes he used to tell, the way he would sing even though he could hardly carry a tune..."

Shane pulled her into a tight embrace, though he knew that he was a poor substitute. "I wish it had been me."

With a small gasp, she pulled away. "Don't say that, Shane. I don't think Jake would have survived losing you."

I've barely survived losing him, he thought. But she didn't want to hear that. "Are you doing anything for the anniversary this year?"

"No, nothing big. I'm sure his father will drink himself into oblivion. I think I'll spend the day with my mother, watching old home movies, looking at pictures." She sniffled and wiped her cheeks. "Next year, I think I'll do something significant."

He nodded, not wanting to assume that he'd be invited. Truthfully, he wasn't sure that he could stomach being in attendance. "Take care of yourself, Missus Talbot."

"You too, Shane. You too."

Light footsteps retreated and he dared not look back at her, not wanting to risk tears of his own spilling onto his cheeks. As he sat down, hand pressed to the menu, he took in a shuddering breath. What little appetite he had was now dissipated.

10

Furrowing his brow as the phone vibrated in his pocket, he couldn't imagine who would be texting him so early. Pulling it from his pocket, he looked at the screen to see that it was his boss.

We're closed today and possibly tomorrow.

Depends on how bad my hangover is.

Enjoy the day off.

Fuck. He'd been counting on work for a distraction. It seemed like today was a bad day for several people, though he had to wonder what Peter's reasons were.

I can work the shop by myself tomorrow, Pete.

Heaving a sigh, he leaned against the front door. The phone vibrated again.

Thanks, kid. Have a good weekend.

Shane pursed his lips. To respond or to leave it be? He didn't want to be a total dick and ignore someone in pain, but, at the same time, he didn't want to get involved. There was enough on his mind without throwing in more complications. The less people around him, the better.

If he ignored them, they would eventually take the hint.

If he acted like a normal, decent human being, and like he gave a shit, they would want to be around him.

There was no way to win in this scenario.

Knowing he might regret this later, he sent a response.

Do you need some company?

The address to Peter's house followed.

Licking his lips, his gaze fell to Teddy, who was fast asleep on his dog bed. He hated leaving him, but he was aging, and it might be best not to bring him. Besides, Teddy would be his excuse to leave when the social aspect got to be too much.

It took forty minutes to reach Peter's house. It always surprised him that the place was modest. For some reason, he'd imagined the ultimate bachelor pad. This looked like the kind of place to raise a family. Maybe that had been the original intention before his son had died.

Shane knocked on the door and it opened almost instantly, as if Pete had been waiting there for him.

"Come on in, kid. Grab a drink. There's pizza too but it's cold now."

Stepping inside, Peter closed the door behind him and Shane followed the unsteady man into the kitchen. It was tempting to go for the alcohol, but it wasn't even noon yet. That made him wonder about the pizza; it must have been from last night. It wasn't hard to believe that the days might be blurring together for Peter, considering the smell wafting from his pores.

"Want anything?"

"No, thanks." Shane shook his head. "I just wanted to check on you, man."

"Oh, I'm fine. Never better!" He chuckled while taking a swig from what appeared to be an empty beer bottle. Pete didn't seem to notice. "Wish I could say the same thing about my kid."

"Oh." This was about his kid again. Not that he thought that kind of pain ever went away; just a few days ago, he had seen Missus Talbot and time had not been kind to her. The stress of losing her child had aged her prematurely. People coped in different ways, Missus Talbot internationalizing her stress in ways that made her age, and Peter drinking to dull his senses. "Is this because of what I said at the shop?"

To him, it looked as though his boss's benders came in phases, as though something had brought them on. While he didn't know what else the man had going on in his personal life, Shane couldn't help but feel responsible for sending him down the path of destruction this particular time.

"No, no, no." He waved his hand before setting the empty bottle on the counter. "This is just what I do. You're not responsible for my actions."

Shane nodded slowly, gaze wandering over him. Though his words were slurred, he had no trouble deciphering them. "Just checking. I know that I can be a shit sometimes. Most of the time. People think I'm not aware of that, but I am."

"Fuck people. You do what you've got to do to survive, mmkay?"

"You don't have to be nice to me, Pete. I know I hurt your feelings. You should let me have it."

"Nice try." He pointed to Shane's chest. "You've got enough to worry about without me adding to your stress."

He shifted uncomfortably, wishing that Peter had never been privy to that information. Luckily, he didn't have to dwell on it as he was being summoned into the living room.

There were what appeared to be children's drawings, cards that showed wear on the edges, and some photo albums.

"I've been looking at these for days," Pete said hoarsely. "I should probably put them away before I get them dirty."

"Here, let me help." He waited for his boss's nod of permission before touching the precious sentiments.

Shane started with the child's drawings, and then organized the cards, before moving to the open photo albums. "Where do you want-" Furrowing his brow, he peered at the second album, one that was filled with a boy who looked to be in his early teens. A boy that was familiar to him.

His fingers brushed one of the photos, mouth dry as he looked up at Peter.

"Who is this?"

It was a question he was afraid of knowing the answer to, though it was simple enough to put together now. He just needed confirmation. The anticipation of Peter's response made his knees buckle, adrenaline already spiking.

"That's him." He pursed his lips, stepping closer to the table to peer at the picture. "That's my son, Jake."

Jake Talbot. His first boyfriend. The person who had changed everything.

"They never found him, you know," Pete continued, his voice breaking. "So we just mark the day of his disappearance as the date of his death. He was so angry with me about the divorce, he wasn't speaking to me at the time. I never got to say goodbye." He choked back a sob. "Jake disappeared on what would have been my weekend if I'd forced him to honor the custody agreement, but I didn't want to force him to see me, you know? Maybe if I had, he'd still be alive..."

"Don't say that." Shane placed a gentle hand on Peter's shoulder and could feel his body shaking from the sobs.

"You were trying to be respectful of his personal space. It's not your fault. I can see how much you loved him."

Bile rose in his throat as he backed away from the table, trying desperately not to make his symptoms of panic obvious. This was too much for him to process and he wasn't ready for his boss to know why.

"I'm sorry, Peter, I've got to go." He slipped his hands into the pockets of his jeans to stop them from shaking. "I have a dog, he's waiting for me."

"Oh, alright." He closed one of the albums before turning to Shane. "I'll see you tomorrow."

"You're taking the day off, remember?"

"Right, right." Peter nodded, even though he'd clearly forgotten. "You probably should too, kiddo. You look really pale."

"Probably coming down with something."

Before that bile reached his tongue and expelled from his lips, Shane rushed out the door and got into his car.

It was wrong to leave Peter in such a state, and alone, but he couldn't stay there. How had he not figured this out before? Granted, Jake had never mentioned his father and he'd never seen any pictures. Since Shane had issues with his own father, he hadn't forced the subject.

Now, he wished that he had. Because, like Peter had said, maybe spending time with his father would have spared Jake. His disappearance had haunted Shane for years, but it couldn't possibly compare to the pain that his parents felt.

That was why he had to stay away from Peter now as well. It would end badly, just like everything else in his life.

His first thought was to text Callan because he needed the comfort, but he'd burned that bridge, though not without good reason. One way or another, everything around him was destroyed. That was why he needed to keep his distance. If he was lucky, he could slowly fade away without anyone realizing it, and spare everyone the misfortune of experiencing what happened when people got too close to him.

Even though he knew that he'd pay for it later, Shane needed a distraction. If he didn't drink himself into oblivion, he might do something much worse.

He spent hours at a local bar, one he'd rarely frequented because of his medication. Alcohol and heart failure didn't mix well.

Voices became garbled around him as he placed his arms on the table and buried his head in them. The bartender was telling him to call a cab but he could barely lift his cell phone, let alone call for a ride and physically leave the bar.

"Hey, Shane. Long time no see."

The voice was a familiar one. Raising his head to make eye contact with Troy, he scrunched his noise. "Whaddo you want?"

"I'm off-duty. Let me take you home."

He shook his head as bile rose in his throat. "No fucking way."

"It's rotten work, but someone's got to do it. Come on."

Troy held out his hand. Shane knew that he wouldn't be able to walk by himself, but he was still hesitant to take it.

"M-my tab."

"I paid for it already."

He pursed his lips, mouth watering as he got to his feet. "Mmkay."

Troy was one of his least favorite people in the world now – and Shane had to be pretty low on Troy's totem pole too – and yet, here he was, being helpful. He didn't know what to make of that.

The car ride was a blur. Thankfully, Troy didn't need to ask where he lived or where the key to the apartment was.

"What the-" Troy stumbled backward as a large German Shepard jumped on him. "Since when do you have a dog?"

"Long story," Shane mumbled as he gave Teddy a gentle pet. "Would you mind taking him outside? I don't think I can make it up and down those stairs again."

"Sure thing."

While they were outside, Shane put food and water in Teddy's bowls, and the effort made him feel so nauseous that he leaned over the counter. He tried and failed to think of anything except the immense sensation.

By the time Troy came back inside, vomit was pooled at Shane's feet, his body shaking from the effort.

"Jesus!" Troy exclaimed. "I can't leave you alone for a minute, can I?"

"S-sorry." He stood at the counter, at a loss for where to begin with the clean-up.

"Don't move, I'll take care of it."

"No, don't." But he was in no position to argue.

Stepping away from the vomit, he used the counter for support, trying to pull off his shoes at the same time. The room started spinning and he groaned, bringing a hand to his forehead.

"Shane. I told you not to move! I don't want you to fall and hurt yourself, especially not when you're on blood thinners."

The rest was a blur, as if he was going in and out of consciousness. Shane's situation wasn't dire, he just couldn't remember how he'd gotten from the kitchen to his bed, and vomit-free. When he realized how clean he felt, he gasped, sitting up in the bed.

"Hey, hey, calm down," Troy spoke softly. "I need to

know what you took. Your heart-rate was freakishly low while you were out, and now it's racing."

"I didn't take anything," he mumbled in response. "Just my pills. And you saw what I drank."

"Is this normal for someone in your condition?"

"Why do you care?" He sighed, settling back down onto the mattress. "We're not friends anymore."

"I still care. Believe me, I wish I didn't."

There was a long pause and Shane knew exactly why, but he thought if they didn't discuss it, they could pretend it hadn't happened.

Taking in a shaky breath, he pulled the blankets over his fresh clothing. Troy had changed him. He had seen Shane's bare skin.

"Shane," he said in a low tone. "I don't understand what I saw."

"Why the fuck does everyone insist on invading my privacy?"

"I didn't mean to, I was just trying to help."

"Yeah, Cal said the same thing."

He furrowed his brow. "Cal knows about those?"

Heaving a sigh, he pulled the blanket over his head. "Go away. Please."

"I can't. It may not be my place to ask, but I can't pretend I didn't see." Troy pulled back the covers to see Shane's face. "How did you get those scars? They don't..." He licked his lips. "They don't make sense, Shane."

"They're not supposed to. I did them myself."

"All of it?" he asked with an incredulous tone.

"It was before you knew me."

Troy chewed his bottom lip, gaze wandering over the length of the bed. "I assume you have a history of mental illness. Is that why you're so guarded?"

"I don't have a mental illness." He paused, knowing that he needed to clarify. "I mean, I'm not on any medication for anything other than my heart."

"Okay, sorry, I didn't mean to offend you." His tone was sincere, softer and quieter than it had ever been before. He was treading carefully. "Were you mentally ill when you cut yourself?"

"I guess so. I just..." Shane covered his face with his hand. "I don't have a good excuse."

"You don't need an excuse to be sad, Shane. It just happens."

"I hated myself so much," he croaked.

The alcohol had blurred the walls he'd built around himself, muddling everything together, making the boundary unclear. He desperately wanted to say something meaningful, something that would mend the broken fence between them. But it was better to leave it broken.

For the briefest of moments, Troy's hand rested on his arm. "Do you still think about hurting yourself?"

"No. There's no point." He shrugged. "I'm going to die anyway."

"Is that true?"

Shane nodded slowly. Uncovering his face, he could see tears in Troy's eyes.

"Man, why does it have to be like this? If your time is limited, why do you have to push everyone away?" He threw his hands in the air. "Why can't you just let us be there for you?"

Shane threw off the blanket, legs swinging over the side of the bed, threatening to get up. "Because I want to be alone!"

Troy raised his hands and stepped away, encouraging him to stay put.

"Fine. If that's what you want."

Shane got back under the covers, pulling them up to his chin. He heard the front door close and the aging German Shepard trotted into the bedroom, whining at him.

"I didn't mean you, buddy." He motioned for Teddy to come closer. The dog sat beside the bed and Shane gave his ears a good scratch. "I know, I was too hard on him. And on Cal. It's for the best, don't you think?"

Scooting over, he patted the spot next to him. "It's not safe with me, big guy. You know that first-hand. What choice do I have?"

Teddy happily curled up on the bed and Shane gently wrapped his arms around him. Sniffling, he closed his eyes and nuzzled Teddy's fur. "Please don't leave me."

THERE WAS A KNOCK AT THE DOOR. IF HE HADN'T successfully alienated everyone in his life, he needed to try harder.

Forcing himself out of bed, he grunted from the effort, hand curling around his sore stomach. He could see that the vomit from the kitchen had been cleaned. How could he thank someone he never planned to see again? That was going to be a tricky thing to navigate, wanting to push people away, and then feeling obligated to show his appreciation when they were kind.

The door opened and in came his mother was bags full of food.

"Um, hello to you too, mom."

He shut the door and went into the kitchen, sitting on the bar stool at the counter..

"Shane Coulter, what have you been up to? You look

like..." She set the bags down on the counter, pursing her lips.

"Like death?"

Lorraine clicked her tongue. "Don't say that. It's not funny."

It wasn't unusual to make jokes about his health. That was just the way he did things. However, he did try to be a little more sensitive around the woman who gave him life.

Panting could be heard from the hallway, and in no time at all, a barking Teddy was at Lorraine's feet.

"Well, hello there!" She smiled and leaned down to pet the fluffy animal. "Is this who I think it is?"

"It's Teddy."

"Cal told me he was looking for him. I can't believe he found him after all this time! I guess he was meant to be with you."

"Yeah. He still likes me, for some reason."

Lorraine unpacked what was in the bags; soup in a carry-out container, crackers, juice, and microwave popcorn. "I had an inkling you weren't feeling well, so I brought your favorites."

He clenched his jaw. "Did Troy tell you?"

"So what if he did?"

"Why can't anyone stay out of my fucking business?"

She clicked her tongue. "Don't swear in my presence. You know I hate cursing."

Heaving a sigh, he threw his head back. "Nothing stays mine anymore. The people I know keep reporting to other people I know. It's frustrating."

"Well, that's because we're all worried about you." She pushed the soup toward him with a spoon from his kitchen drawer. "Me, Troy, Cal, even..."

He pursed his lips, waiting for her to finish.

"Your brother too."

"Ethan's not speaking to me right now. And I'm not speaking to Troy. Or Cal." He opened the container, stirring the contents with the spoon.

"Sweetheart, you can't shut everyone out." She leaned against the counter. "Are you going to stop talking to me next?"

"Yeah," he mumbled, although he had trouble making eye-contact. "If you can't respect my boundaries."

"If you have a problem with everyone in your life, honey...the problem is you."

His nostrils flared, but he knew she was right. "Thanks for your honesty, mom."

"I'm only saying this because I love you." She walked around the counter and placed a kiss on top of his head. "You have to work on how you communicate. It doesn't come across well."

"It's just my personality. I'm not going to change just because people don't like me."

"We love you, Shane."

"Yeah, but no one *likes* me."

Sighing softly, Lorraine combed her fingers through his hair. "You could try to compromise. At least a smidge."

He shook his head. "No. This is how I live now."

"Can't blame me for trying."

Turning on his stool, he wrapped his arms around her. "Thanks for coming, mom."

She gently rubbed his back. "Shane, have you thought about talking to someone? Professionally, I mean."

"They can't help me. No one can."

"Promise me you'll reach out to someone. Anyone." Stepping back, she lifted his chin so that he would look at her. "Everyone needs *someone*. And no matter how tough you act, you're lonely. I can see it in your eyes."

He shrugged, sliding off the stool. "I'm better off alone."

OPENING THE DOOR, HE ALLOWED HIS LESS-THAN-ENTHUSED guest inside. Against his better judgment, Shane had asked Callan to join him for the evening.

Teddy barked, tail wagging excitedly as Cal bent down to pet him.

"So, is this guy your new excuse for never coming to *my* place?"

"Hey, I was there...once." Shane pursed his lips, foolishly thinking his sort-of boyfriend hadn't caught on to that avoidance. "I don't feel safe anywhere but here."

"I can understand that." After letting the dog give him a lick, he stood up straight, towering over the brunette. "What I *don't* understand is what happened the last time I was here."

Tension hung in the air. Callan was annoyed – had every right to be, but the look on his face expressed something close to anger. That was something he'd never seen from his lover before. His immediate reaction was to take a step back and lower his gaze.

"I want to apologize," he spoke in a low tone.

"Hey, I'm not gonna-" Furrowing his brow, he took a step closer, and Shane took another step back. "Are you afraid of me?"

"No." He forced himself to look at Cal. "I'm sorry, okay? I was upset and I shouldn't have taken it out on you."

"Do you have any idea how hurtful that was?" Closing his eyes, he shook his head. "We made love. It was a beautiful experience for me. Best birthday I've ever had. And then, suddenly, you were kicking me out." He opened his mouth and closed it again. When he spoke next, his voice was unsteady. "I just want to understand what was going through your mind. I never meant to push you into doing something you didn't want to do."

"That's not why I was angry." Shane heaved a sigh. "Making love to you...I think that was the best night of my life."

"So what changed? Is it because I saw your scars and you didn't want me to?"

He shrugged. "Some."

"Because you're ashamed of them?"

Shane wrung his hands together to prevent them from shaking. This line of questioning was dangerous and he needed to change the subject quickly, or he might crack under the pressure. "You don't understand, Cal."

"Then help me."

Cal held out his hand but Shane couldn't take it. He hadn't been taking his pills regularly and now it was coming back to bite him in the ass. "Give me a minute."

Rushing into the bathroom, he opened the cabinet, fumbling around the shelves to find the right bottles, even though he knew exactly where they were. His mind was in a fog, vision blurring as he attempted to steady his breathing.

Taking the handful of medications, he turned on the sink, cupping water into his hands and swallowing everything in one gulp. Hands gripping the porcelain, he took several deep breaths in an effort to lower his heart rate.

Shutting off the faucet, he then turned around only to be met by Cal in the doorway. His jaw was clenched.

"What are you taking?"

"Vitamins."

"That come in a prescription bottle?"

"Yeah, really strong ones. I'm very depleted."

Shane pushed past him and wandered back into the kitchen area.

Callan followed him and stood at the door, hand on the knob. "You're lying to me."

Licking his lips anxiously, Shane approached him cautiously, as if any fast movements might spook him. "Cal, don't leave. Please."

"How can I stay when you're not being honest with me?"

Slowly, Shane wrapped his arms around the much taller man, reaching on his tip-toes to place a kiss against his neck. "Stay."

"That's awfully manipulative." Cal sighed exasperatedly, hands gently gripping Shane's shoulders. "You're trying to use my feelings for you to your advantage because you know I'll melt like butter."

He grinned while slipping off Cal's coat. "That's not what I'm doing."

Cal tried to hide a small smile. "Then enlighten me."

"I just want to be with you."

"Goddamn it, Shane." Eyes brimming with tears, he moved his hands to Shane's cheeks. "Do you have any idea how precious you are to me?"

"I know." Shane's arms tightened around him. "And I don't deserve your love, Callan."

"You still believe that? Is that what all this back and forth is about?"

He lowered his gaze. "I have my reasons."

"I'm sure you do. But you can't keep doing this." A hand brushed through Shane's curls. "Not to me, not to your friends and family, and not to yourself."

"Can't we leave everyone else out of this? Can't it just be the two of us?"

"That's not realistic." He paused. "Unless you're saying that you want our relationship to be a secret."

"No, that's not-" Shane clicked his tongue, bunching up the back of Callan's shirt in his hands. "I'm not ashamed of you, if that's what you're thinking. I'm just trying to protect you."

"From what?"

"From the world. And me."

He furrowed his brow and tilted his head. "Are you dangerous, Shane?"

"I don't want to hurt you, Cal. But I can't promise that I won't." Releasing Cal's shirt, he took a step backward. "It's what I do. People get hurt because of me."

Gaze wandering over him, the blond was silent for a moment while he assessed the other. Shoulders slumping in defeat, he pulled Shane into a gentle embrace. "I don't know about tomorrow, or next week, or next month, but, tonight, I love you too much to leave. So, I'll stay."

"That's fair." He closed his eyes and nuzzled Cal's chest. "I won't blame you for leaving. Now or ever."

THE HUSTLE AND BUSTLE OF THE MALL MADE HIS NOSE scrunch. Christmas was rapidly approaching and people were doing their shopping. He just wanted to do his *regular* shopping. The holiday had lost its luster years ago. Come to think of it, he couldn't remember the last holiday he'd been genuinely excited about. Even as a child, the thrill had never been there.

When Harper and Hayden were born, it had made Christmas appealing. They were a joy to be around, always cheerful, getting him into holiday activities, being so grateful for even the smallest gift.

Now that he wasn't allowed to see them, this time of year had become meaningless again. Although Ethan and Nora had promised to be civil during their family gathering, Shane had doubts about attending. It was better to let them have their fun without him spoiling it.

They had managed Thanksgiving without him; they could manage Christmas too. Except, on the last holiday, he had asked Peter if he could occupy himself at the shop. Peter, who liked to drink, especially during any holidays, hadn't minded, and Shane had been provided with a distraction.

This time would be different. He'd been staying far away from Peter and the shop in the same way he'd been distancing himself from everything and everyone else. Slowly but surely, he was taking less shifts, letting his boss and friend believe that it was because of his heart. He felt like shit about misleading Peter, especially about his health, but it wasn't too far from the truth.

Gaze glued to his phone, he walked down the halls, passing various shops and bumping shoulders with strangers he didn't care enough to apologize to. Then a voice of protest was one that he recognized.

"That's a safety hazard, you know."

Shane placed the phone in his pocket and looked up to see his brother. Though Ethan's face was as warm and kind as ever, it made him feel small.

"Well, we don't all have families to occupy our time," he quipped.

"You could if you wanted to."

"Uncle Shane!" Harper and Hayden came running out from one of the nearby stores.

"Hey, guys!" An immediate grin spread across his cheeks and he knelt down and opened his arms for them. The children hugged him tightly and he blinked away the tears forming in his eyes. "I miss you."

"We miss you too." Harper pulled away, pouting her bottom lip. "Why didn't you come to Thanksgiving? Did we do something wrong?"

His heart sank and he attempted to swallow the lump in his throat. "No, of course not. I had to work, that's all."

"Will you be at grandma's house for Christmas?" Hayden tilted his head curiously.

Now his heart was aching where it had sunk. He didn't want to lie to them, but he didn't want to ruin the holiday for them either. They didn't understand, but it would happen one way or another. And he wasn't going to throw Ethan and Nora under the bus. Even though they may have been the reason he wouldn't attend, it was his behavior that had led to this situation. "I'm going to try. I have presents for you both, so I'll leave them under grandma's tree just in case."

Harper furrowed her brow. "We don't care about presents, Uncle Shane. We just want to see you."

The growing lump in his throat made it difficult to speak. "I love you guys. You know that, right?"

"We love you too."

They each gave him a hug before he stood up. "Call me any time. Even if I'm working, I'll pick up. Just don't tell my boss."

He winked and they giggled.

Nora smiled politely as she joined them, arm looping around her husband's. "Hey, Shane. How're you doing?"

"I'm okay, Nora. Thanks for asking."

Making sure the kids were out of ear-shot, she then looked him over. "You don't *look* okay."

Narrowing his gaze, he shook his head, at a loss for

words. Couldn't win, could he? If he spent time with them, they were angry, but if he stayed away, they were worried. "Why do you care, Nora?" Peering over her shoulder to make sure Harper and Hayden were busy going through their shopping bags, he lowered his voice. "I don't blame you for kicking me out of your lives, and theirs, but don't act like you give a shit about how it's affecting me."

She opened her mouth to speak but Ethan stepped between them. "You did this, Shane. You can't blame other people for the consequences of your actions."

With a wave of his hand, he turned on his heel and continued down the hall, though didn't get very far before he felt a grip on his shoulder.

"Do you think it's fair, what you're doing to my kids?"

Shrugging off his brother's hand, his nostrils flared as he faced him. "What do you mean?"

"You heard them." Ethan scoffed and shook his head. "They miss you, and yet, you won't make the necessary changes to see them."

Shane swallowed hard, gaze drifting toward his brother's family. They looked happy, blissfully unaffected by his behavior. For them, all was as it should be, and that was how he wanted it to remain. "They know that I love them. That's all that matters."

For a moment, it looked as though something spiteful might be on the tip of Ethan's tongue. And then his features softened, as if rethinking his response. "Nora's right. You don't look well. What's going on with you?"

"Nothing." Shane didn't want to tell him about his discovery – that Peter had turned out to be Jake Talbot's father. Ethan wouldn't understand what it meant and why it was so significant. "I'm respecting your boundaries, Ethan. You need to respect mine."

"Is it your heart?" He took a step closer. "Did something happen?"

"No, my condition hasn't changed." His hands rose like a signal to tell Ethan to back off. "I'm fine."

"I don't know why you keep saying that when it's clear that you're not."

It was surprising that his brother could see through the facade. If people could see the cracks in the walls he'd built around himself, that was fine, just as long as they didn't know why the cracks had appeared. "Trying to will it into existence, I guess. If I keep saying it, one day, it might be true."

There was a long pause. Ethan licked his lips anxiously, gaze wandering over Shane, even opening and closing his mouth twice before actually speaking. "I know you're going to regret this someday, but you're my brother, and I love you, so I don't want you to beat yourself up over it. Even though I'll never understand the choices you're making, I'll admit that I've never been in your position, so I don't know how it feels." Pursing his lips, his gaze lowered. "If this is how you have to deal with it, I can't blame you or tell you that it's wrong. I don't believe that this is the right way to handle your problems, but, clearly, you do."

Shane hated everything about this moment – how he felt so defeated, how Ethan *looked* so defeated. Both of them struggling to find a connection, some miraculous link that would bring them back together and make everything alright again. To anyone who didn't know the truth, it seemed like an easy fix. But to Shane, it was hopeless. He wouldn't lift a finger to be welcomed back into Ethan's life, and that of his niece and nephew, because he wholeheartedly believed that they were better off without him.

Realizing that Shane wouldn't respond, Ethan heaved a sigh. "I love you, man. I hope you see the light one day."

"Don't count on it."

As his brother walked away, looking the saddest that Shane had ever seen him, he cleared his throat. "Hey, Ethan-"

Ethan stopped.

"I love you too."

He nodded slowly. "I know."

Rejoining his family, Ethan wrapped his arms around the three of them and they disappeared into one of the many stores in the mall.

Shane stood still, not minding the flurry of people walking past him, some giving him strange looks as he was the only person not moving.

He was trying to memorize the image of Ethan, Harper, Hayden, and even Nora. An image that would remind him of the very reason he was staying away from them. They were happy. They loved one another in ways that he would never be able to experience because he would never have a spouse, or children, and any of the memories they were making as a family.

The thought of the family of four being safe and happy would bring him great comfort. It would ease the pain of not seeing them. And he prayed to God that they would never understand his reasoning.

Shane wouldn't be able to bear it if they had known the truth.

11

The holiday was just a few days away, and because he had made it perfectly clear that he would not be in attendance, Lorraine had insisted on making him a private meal. How could he say no to his mother's cooking?

"It's ready!" she called from the kitchen.

He arranged a few extra gifts under the Christmas tree for Harper and Hayden. While he tried not to play favorites with the people in his life, his niece and nephew certainly received the largest stack of gifts.

Shane placed a kiss on his mother's cheek before sitting at the table. They were quiet while eating the roast and potatoes. He wondered what meal would be cooked for Ethan. It wasn't that he was bitter about it, he just knew what he would be missing out on. Time. He was wasting it, throwing it away as if it was insignificant.

Time was the only thing he'd been able to count on. Time passing. Time wasted. Time spent. Time stolen. Everything was measured in time; in minutes and hours. Life was made up of moments big and small, disappointing and surprising, heart-breaking and joyful.

Time was always there. It could not be ignored; he was so aware of it. He doubted that anyone knew just how much he paid attention to it.

Its passage hadn't brought him the peace he had sought. All he could think about was the time he'd had, the time he hadn't, and all the time that was taken for granted. Time that he was fortunate enough to have where others did not.

Maybe that was why he took comfort in the fact that, for him, time was limited. It would run out. One way or another, Shane wouldn't live to see a ripe, old age of anything. His death would approach more quickly than that of the average person, certainly more quickly than someone his age should expect.

Those were the only two things he could count on: time and death, for they were both certain. Everything else was a guessing game, and he hated not knowing what was going to happen – or when.

The ticking of his mother's grandfather clock grew louder in his ears, counting every second he was lucky to be alive. And he hated every minute of it. It was a reminder that others had not been so lucky, like Jacob Talbot.

He wouldn't have been so ungrateful. Jake probably would have given anything to be enjoying a meal with his family.

"Your father stopped by the other day."

Shane dropped his fork. "Why was he here?"

Clicking her tongue, she picked the utensil off the floor and then went into the kitchen to fetch another.

"He said that he wants to see you," her voice carried across the rooms. "But he doesn't want to make you uncomfortable by showing up on your doorstep. So he showed up on mine." She smiled and handed him a new fork before sitting down again. "Do you have any interest in talking to him again?"

"No," he said through gritted teeth.

"Now, Shane, what happened between your father and I..." She trailed off, taking a deep breath. "That's between us. You shouldn't hold a grudge against him for something he did to me, you know, twenty-something years ago."

"I'm twenty-four," he reminded her. "And, yes, I can. You're my mother. There's no excuse."

"I knew he had a wandering eye and I got involved with him anyway. I thought he might change but I should have known that he wouldn't."

"You haven't dated anyone since he cheated on you. If his actions affected you that badly then I don't want to be around him."

"I never should have told you that he was unfaithful." She sighed and brushed her fingers through his messy curls. "You might still have a relationship if you hadn't known. He loves you, Shane. You should give him another chance. He hurt *me*, not you. I don't want you to distance yourself from him on my account. I'm your mother and it's my job to encourage a relationship between the two of you."

Shane folded his arms. "I don't want to see him and that's that."

"Honey, is it because of your scars? You don't have to be ashamed of them. That's all in the past now."

"Maybe for you. But for me, it never ends."

"What are you saying?" She furrowed her brow. "Shane, should I be worried?"

"No." His nostrils flared. "I'm not going to hurt myself. It's just embarrassing that everyone knows about the worst time in my life. There are some things I want to keep private, okay? I want to be able to move on, to live a normal life, to be happy. And I can't be if the rest of you are so hellbent on reminiscing about the past and who I used to be instead of accepting me for who I am now."

"Oh, sweetheart." Lorraine kissed his forehead. "I'm so sorry. I didn't understand."

She gave him an extra scoop of potatoes while he blinked away the tears in his eyes.

"I'll do better, Shane. Alright? We won't talk about your scars again, I promise."

CALLAN PULLED HIM CLOSER AS THE SCARIEST PART OF THE movie played out on the TV screen. The sounds were frightening Teddy so he turned it down, not even aware that Shane had averted his gaze for similar reasons.

"What do you want for Christmas?" he asked gently.

"Nothing."

He clicked his tongue. "Everyone says that, but everyone wants *something*."

Shane shook his head. "I mean it, Cal. Don't buy me anything."

Pulling back, he furrowed his brow. "Is this a test?"

"No, I'm being completely serious." He turned to face Callan properly. "I don't want...I can't handle..." Taking a deep breath, he folded his arms, unable to complete the thought.

"What is it?" Cal nudged his arm. "Tell me. I won't get upset, I promise."

"I don't like it when people spend money on me. It just makes me feel...icky. Sometimes it makes me literally sick. I can't stomach it."

"I had no idea." Cal rubbed his back soothingly. "What brought that on?"

"I don't know. No one's ever made me feel like I owe them or anything like that. But that's how I feel anyway, indebted to anyone who buys me something, especially when I ask them not to." Lying was like second nature to him, and he hated that he could do it so easily with his lover. It made him feel like the scum of the earth. Callan had always been too good to him, even at his worst. "My family doesn't understand it either. They get upset about it."

"I'm not upset. If it bothers you that much, I won't buy you anything." He pursed his lips, gaze wandering over Shane. "That has to come from somewhere, though. Maybe you just don't remember."

He cleared his throat uncomfortably. Not only was Cal smarter than he would have liked, but could always see right through him too. He was just too polite to call Shane a liar. "Well, I was court-ordered to see my dad. I didn't have a say. And it's not like he's a horrible person, I've just always hated being forced into things. People would tell me that I owed my father my time because, you know, he raised me, paid the bills and all that shit."

"I can see why that would affect you now." He tilted his head, hand absentmindedly petting the dog who was seated against the couch. "I don't really understand why that would bother you if you had a good relationship with your father."

Shane's breath hitched in his throat. "I mean, he didn't do anything to me, it just...it was like my mother, I guess. He wasn't very open-minded. It affected me to the point where I don't have a relationship with him anymore." Heaving a sigh, his palm wiped his face. "My mom was a little different because of Ethan. Eventually, she changed. So, I let her back into my life. My dad, not so much."

"It's very brave of you to walk away from people who are mistreating you." With a soft smile, he rested his head on

Shane's shoulder. "Not everyone has the strength to do that."

Even though he was certain that Cal had an inkling he was lying through his teeth, he still managed to be sweet and supportive. It made Shane feel sick. The more he thought about it, the more nauseous he felt. "I'm not brave, Cal. I'm a fucking coward. I walk away from people who are *good* to me too."

They were soon unable to keep their eyes open and headed to bed. Teddy curled up on his bed in the corner of the room and the three of them were fast asleep in no time at all.

In the early hours of the morning, Shane began to whimper. The familiar sound woke Cal, however, it was not unusual, so he pulled Shane closer and attempted to fall back asleep.

Just as he started to drift off again, a hand collided with his face.

"Jesus!" Sitting up, he realized that Shane was still asleep, and thrashing wildly. "Shane, wake up! You're having a nightmare!"

He was no longer whimpering but screaming, hand smacking Callan in the face several times while he attempted to hold Shane down.

"Shane!" Cal shook him, trying to subdue him and not cause injury in the process. "Wake up! *Wake up!*"

Silence. All movement ceased. Shane was wheezing, trying to catch his breath as he slowly sat against his pillows.

"What happened?" he whispered.

"You tell *me*."

Flicking on the lamp on the bedside table, Cal's face was illuminated in the light, and Shane could see that his face was red and lip was bleeding.

"Fuck, Cal, did I...did *I* do that to you?"

"Yeah." Sitting back, he folded his arms. "Are you going to tell me why?"

"I-" He swallowed hard, hand wiping his face. "I'm so sorry, Cal. I never meant to hurt you."

"Well, I guess you did warn me, didn't you?"

"That's not what I meant."

"What *did* you mean?"

"Fuck." Resting his head in his hands, Shane's fingernails dug into his skull.

"Hey, don't do that!" Callan forced Shane's fingers away from his scalp. "I know this is bad, but it's not worth bleeding out over."

His breathing had steadied but he couldn't find the words to explain what his nightmare had involved.

"Shane, you owe me an explanation," he said in a tone that was not kind. "I mean, I *deserve* an explanation."

All he could do was shake his head, and that prompted Cal to plant his feet on the floor.

"Alright, you've won. This game we're playing – I can't do it anymore. You love me one minute and hate me the next." Teddy whined as Cal lingered near the door, hand on his forehead. "I know that I broke your heart, and I could understand if this was your way of revenge. You keep insisting that it isn't, that it's you and not me, but how can I not take it personally?"

"I know," he stated quietly. "I'm sorry."

"But not sorry enough to be honest with me."

He threw his hands in the air. "It's not all *about* you!"

"No, you're right. It's all about what *you* want, and what *you* need. You wanted to push me away, right? That was the goal?" Cal carefully wiped the blood from his lip. "Well, you've succeeded."

Shane averted his gaze. "This wasn't a game for me."

"Wasn't it? If you didn't take pleasure in the constant back and forth, the tug of war, then why were we doing it?"

"Because that's how I am now! That's how I deal with all the bullshit!" Throwing Teddy an apologetic look for the raised voices, he attempted to lower his own. "I'm sorry that I'm not a better person, okay? I'm sorry that I can't be like you."

Cal scoffed, shaking his head. "I never asked you to change. I only ever asked for the truth."

"You don't fucking know what it's like."

"You think I haven't struggled? That's *all* I've done."

"Yeah, you're not the only one."

"The difference is that I tell you about mine. That way, you can understand *why* I am the way that I am."

Shane heaved a sigh, still avoiding his lover's gaze, and the cut on his lip. "Like I said, I can't be like you."

Bottom lip trembling, Cal wiped his eyes. "Fine. I'm not going to be your punching bag anymore. I love you, but I won't let you destroy me."

He shot the taller man a glare. "You don't know what it's like to be destroyed."

"How long am I supposed to ignore this?"

Shane stared at him wearily. "What?"

"The shaking. The cold sweats in the middle of the night. The pills. The nosebleeds."

"You still think I'm an addict, huh?"

"I don't know what to think because you won't tell me."

Pursing his lips, he thought about brushing off the question once again, but knew that if he didn't answer this time, he might lose the love of his life. "I'm sick."

The look on Callan's face was as if someone had just punched him in the gut. "How sick?"

"I was diagnosed when I was sixteen. Heart failure."

"Oh my God..." He swallowed hard, gaze wandering over Shane. "You never said anything. But how could I not have known?"

"I didn't want you to know." Shane shrugged. "I'm very good at keeping secrets."

"I don't want there to be secrets between us." Kneeling at the edge of his bed, Cal placed his hands on the top of Shane's thighs. "I want us to move forward with our relationship, if that's what this is."

"That's what I want it to be." A lump formed in his throat. Tears brimmed his eyes, forcing him to look away. He didn't want Callan to see any display of emotion. "But I don't know if I can do this."

"Why not?" He furrowed his brow. "You don't think you can rely on me?"

"I know I can, I'm just not sure if I want to."

"Why do I feel like I'm still missing something? I don't understand, Shane." Getting to his feet, Cal paced the floor, moving back and forth between Shane's bed and Teddy's. "You either want me or you don't. You either love me or...you don't. I don't know what you want from me."

"I want *everything* from you...*with* you." He gathered the blankets and pulled them to his chest. "But I don't think..."

"What, Shane? What is it?" Getting back into bed, Cal sat beside him, his tone softened. "Tell me, please. I don't want to keep guessing."

Shane still refused to make eye contact. He couldn't bear to look at his handywork. "I don't deserve you."

"Stop saying that. You don't get to make that decision for me. I'm still here, aren't I? If I didn't want to be, I wouldn't." With a soft smile, he rested his hand on Shane's arm. "I'm confused as hell most of the time, but I love you enough to stay. I loved the old you. I love the new you. And I will continue to love you as you change, and as we grow. I choose you, I've chosen you, and I will keep choosing you." He tilted his head, squeezing his arm gently. "So, what's stopping us?"

Shane closed his eyes. "Fear."

"Of what? Of *me*?"

"No."

"Of love?"

"No," he whispered.

"Then what, Shane? Why won't you tell me?"

"I can't," his voice broke. "I just can't."

Cal fell silent, studying him. "I'm not giving up on you."

"Yeah, well, you should. Unless you really want to keep doing this for the rest of our lives."

"What I want is to hold you. What I want is to kiss you. What I want is to love you and keep you safe from any and all harm. So, if you feel the same way, then why won't you let me?"

"Because I have to let you go."

He blinked rapidly. "I don't care that you're sick."

"It's not about that."

"Then what is it? What's *wrong*, Shane?" His tone was desperate.

"Nothing. I can't say that I love you, Callan." Pulling away from Cal's touch, he brought his knees to his chest and wrapped his arms around them. "I can't even say that I *like* you."

"What would I mean if you did?"

It was on the tip of his tongue, and had been more than once since they'd reconnected, but Shane constantly had to remind himself that it wasn't worth the risk. "Neither of us would be safe from the fallout. Just take my word for it, okay?"

There was a long pause, and then, "Those three words that you can't bring yourself to say, is that how you feel about me? You don't have to say it out loud, just nod or shake your head."

I love you, he thought, but simply nodded in response.

"Okay, then I don't need anything else."

Shane had to wonder if that would be enough. That, somehow, by not verbalizing his true feelings, it would keep Callan safe.

Maybe he was overthinking this. Was there even still a danger? The past could come back to haunt him, but was it actually a physical threat?

He needed Cal more than he could ever admit. And, maybe, just maybe, everything would be okay. If Cal didn't mind those three words not being verbalized – as long as he *knew* how Shane felt – there was the possibility that they could have a normal life.

Normal was more than he deserved, but Callan Reid certainly deserved it, and he wanted that with Shane.

If he let go, just a little, and let Cal in, it was possible that his life wouldn't fall apart, that they could be happy and safe. They had to try. After everything they had been through, they owed it to themselves.

"Okay."

Cal smiled. "Okay?"

Shane nodded and Cal pulled him into a gentle embrace.

"I'm going to take care of you, Shane Coulter. You're safe with me."

"That's not what I'm worried about," he mumbled into Cal's chest.

"You and your secrets. I guess I'll have to accept that I will never know them all." Resting his chin on top of the brunette's head, his fingers brushed over soft curls. "I can keep your demons at bay, you just have to let me."

"It's safer if you don't. For both of us." He closed his eyes, arms tightening around his lover. "My demons are much more dangerous than you think."

The morning came too soon and Shane was hardly ready for the day when he rolled out of bed. The other side of it was empty, as was Teddy's bed on the floor.

With a groan, he dragged himself to the kitchen to see that Callan was making breakfast.

"You didn't have to do that," he mumbled. "I'm not very hungry."

"Don't you have to eat when you take your pills?"

He rubbed his tired eyes. "Did you read the bottles or something?"

"No, I just assumed." Cal paused. "I do that a lot. I'm sorry."

"What are you apologizing for? I didn't give you any reason to have faith in me. Secrecy creates suspicion." Approaching slowly, his fingertips grazed Callan's bottom lip. "I'm not innocent in all of this."

"Yes, you are." Cal kissed his fingers. "I know you don't mean the things you do and say."

"I told you that I hurt people whether I intend to or not. It just happens."

"I'm okay, Shane. It's you I'm worried about."

"What? About this old thing?" He patted his chest.

Cal nodded; gaze lowered as he was unable to speak.

"Hey..." Shane wrapped his arms around the tall blond. "Don't cry over me. I'm not worth it."

That was the wrong thing to say because it only made Cal cry harder.

"Shit, sorry. Please don't cry." He pulled him in a bit tighter. "We'll be alright. Except, I won't be if I'm late for work."

"Well, I'll get out of your hair then." Cal wiped his eyes when he pulled away.

"I didn't mean that you had to leave. But I do."

"I should get some work done too." He offered a small smile.

"You still working on the story with the weird connections that don't actually connect?"

Cal chuckled. "Sounds ridiculous when you put it that way. But, no, I wasn't getting anywhere on that one, so I've moved on to something else."

Shane couldn't hide the look of relief on his face. "I'm glad you're doing what you love."

"Now we just need to get *you* writing again."

"That ship has sailed, I think. I'm just happy to have you and Teddy back. That's all I need."

He saw Callan out before feeding Teddy and then going into work. This was going to be an awkward day, mainly because he was contemplating quitting.

Peter might realize that something was going on, but, hopefully, would never find out. Shane didn't want him to know anything. That was how he was able to live his life. As long as no one knew his secrets, he could sleep at night – that is, when the nightmares gave him a break. And that wasn't often.

His secrets allowed him to cling to a false sense of normalcy. Without them, he would fall apart. No good would come of that; not for him or anyone else.

"Have you been avoiding me, kid?"

Looking up from behind the desk, he shrugged. "Maybe."

Seated between two shelves, Peter continued to unpack a box. "Why?"

"Because you keep calling me *kid*."

Peter shot him a look. "Shane, I'm serious. I think something changed after you came to my house."

"Yeah." Clicking on the keyboard, he focused his gaze on the computer monitor. "Something did."

"Are you going to tell me what that was?"

"No, I don't think I will."

"Well, I'm not going to play a guessing game." He heaved a sigh. "Besides, if you really knew what I *think* you do, I'd be hearing about it...knowing you."

Shane narrowed his gaze, now highly suspicious. Peter couldn't possibly know the reason for his avoidance. "And what is it that you *think* I know?"

"I'm not going to tell you." Shane looked up just into time to see Peter's smug smile. "See how that works?"

He scrunched his nose, the smile making him uneasy. "I didn't know it was a competition."

The smile faded as he picked up the now-empty box and set it on the desk. "Was it awkward for you to see me at such a low point?"

"No. I've seen you on bad days."

"Okay, then. I'm at a loss." He pushed the box to the side so that he had a better view of Shane. "I'm trying to figure you out, kid. You sure don't make it easy."

"I'm not a fucking kid." Shane logged out of the computer and grabbed his car keys from the other side of the monitor. "I've been through things that you can't even imagine."

"I don't know about that. I've got a pretty active imagination." He placed his elbows on the desk before interlocking his fingers. "See, when my son died, that's when my imagination really took off. I thought about him being alive, and dead, in the most fucked up ways. When you lose someone, but you don't know what happened to them, that's what your mind does. It plays on your worst fears, conjures up your nightmares and puts them on repeat."

Little did Peter know that Shane had shared those nightmares. He, too, had imagined Jake's suffering in a variety of ways, knowing that any and all of them were his fault. Keys clenched in his fist, he walked out from behind the desk, trying to put as much distance from himself and the older male as possible. "Why are you telling me this?"

"Because I feel like I'm losing you, Shane, and I don't know what happened to you." Peter's voice was the softest that it had ever been. "I don't know why."

While he had suspected it before, this was the moment when he realized how close he and his boss had become, despite his best efforts. This was a failure that he needed to rectify because if Peter learned the truth about what had happened to his son, they would both pay the price. "You never had me."

"Don't you know that you're like a son to me?"

"Ah, so that's it. *That's* why you care about me. You just want a second chance." He shook his head. "Well, it's not going to be with me. I quit."

Tears formed in Peter's eyes which forced Shane to look away. The tightening in his chest was uncomfortable and he needed to get out of this situation before it got worse.

"Shane, it's not like that. I'm not trying to replace Jake. I love him, and I'll always miss him, but he's gone."

He's dead, Shane thought. All color drained from his face when, for a moment, he thought he had said the words out loud. Peter's expression remained the same, and he considered himself lucky, but if he stayed in the presence of Jake's father any longer, that would change.

"Well, so am I, Pete."

Not daring to look at him as he brushed past, Shane pushed the door open and found relief in the silence of his car.

The only thing he could hear was the pumping in his ears from a heart overworked. He wanted to scream, to throw something, but either may result in injury. And that would require yet another hospital visit and more people worrying about it, invading his comfort zone and crossing the boundaries he'd set that had, so far, seemed pointless. Not that he regretted setting them in the first place. That was how he had survived this long.

Groaning softly, he placed a hand to his chest, rubbing it gently. This was going to turn into a sleepless night.

Maybe he could spend the evening with Callan to distract himself from the fact that he was becoming completely unraveled.

Only, being with Cal may be a further reminder of that. Was it worth the risk? That was the question he constantly asked himself. It was the only thing that shielded the ones he loved from harm. That single question had been the safety barrier between life and death. They would never understand and that was alright by him.

If any one of them died because of him, however unintentionally, he would never be able to forgive himself.

They didn't know how dangerous it was to even be in his presence.

Jake Talbot's blood was on his hands.

If he wasn't careful, he may be responsible for the deaths of everyone he held dear. And where would it end?

Family would always be caught in the crossfire, but did the danger extend to romantic relationships? Friends? Friends of friends? Acquaintances?

He should just save everyone the trouble and drive off a cliff. If he was going to abandon them anyway, what was the point?

One action could end all of this.

Except, he couldn't know that for certain. And the pain that he caused wouldn't end even if his life did.

Dying on his own terms was always in the back of his mind, but he had a few karmic debts to pay before he could ever consider it.

Hands gripping the steering while, he looked up to see that Peter had been staring at him through the window.

Shane wondered if it would help his would-be father figure to know that he was losing his mind or if that would make matters worse.

Maybe he actually needed to say the words, 'it's my fault your son is dead', for Peter to stop caring about him.

12

Pursing his lips, he looked down at the ringing phone in his hand. It was Nora. He had half a mind to ignore her because they had never talked before and he didn't see a reason to start now, but she could be calling about something to do with the kids.

So, he answered.

"Did Hell freeze over?"

There was a long pause. "Shane, this is very serious."

He pinched the bridge of his nose, preparing for whatever headache she was about to give him. "Okay."

"Have you seen Ethan?"

"You know I haven't." Thinking it might be a good idea to be slightly less of a pain, he added, "Not since that day at the mall."

"Then I guess it's official. You were my last resort." Her voice was unsteady. "Ethan is missing."

His breath hitched in his throat. "What do you mean he's missing?"

"I mean he's been gone for almost twenty-four hours. I tried to report it sooner, but..."

"Let me guess, the police were no help." He chewed his bottom lip. "Not even for a fellow officer, huh?"

"They wanted me to check every possibility. And now I have." It sounded like Nora was choking back a sob. "You know he wouldn't leave and not tell me where he was going."

"Yeah. I know that, Nora. You guys mean the world to him." Shane closed his eyes. "Is there anything I can do?"

"I'll let you know." She sniffled. "We're going to celebrate Christmas with my parents. Your mother will be with us and you're welcome to come. I don't think it'll work to distract the kids, but...I'm doing the best I can."

Gritting his teeth, he took a deep breath before answering. "I appreciate the invite, but I don't think I'll be able to keep it together for them, you know?"

"I understand. I'm barely able to do it myself."

They should be used to this; him letting them down. But it didn't make him feel any better in doing so. "I'm sorry. I'm really sorry."

"I'll let you know if anything changes."

Nora hung up and he set his phone on the coffee table. Teddy whined, coming closer as Shane curled up on the couch. He tried to control his breathing and failed.

His heart was racing and his breaths were heaving. The medication wouldn't take away these symptoms. Being with his family on Christmas wouldn't make him feel better. Nothing could ease his guilt.

What Nora didn't know was that Shane had been through this before and he knew exactly where it would lead.

With a bit of difficulty, Teddy jumped onto the couch and curled against Shane's body. He felt completely undeserving of such comfort, but couldn't help wrapping an arm around his pet.

"I'm so sorry." His tears mingled with the dog's soft fur. "I never meant for any of this to happen. I try to tell people that they're going to get hurt and they never listen to me. You can't stay here with me or you'll go missing too."

Teddy shifted, groaning disapprovingly.

He sat up and patted Teddy's shoulder. It was pointless to try and wipe away his tears because he couldn't keep up with them.

"I thought it was over. Nothing had happened in such a long time." Pulling his knees to his chest, he took a shaky breath, hands pressed to his temples. "Unless something has...and I just don't know about it. How could I be so fucking stupid?"

Jake's blood was on his hands. And now Ethan's. When would it be enough for him to learn the lesson? It was dangerous to be near him. They were dead and it was his fault.

How long before that number rose? How long before he was responsible for the deaths of each of his loved ones?

He couldn't allow anyone else to die. Whatever it took to alienate them, he had to do it.

Was it worth the risk?

The answer was no. It always had been, yet he'd kept trying.

"I can't do this, Teddy. I fucking can't."

Stepping over the senior, Shane hastily moved toward the kitchen and opened the drawers in search of the sharpest knife.

"I have to stop this before someone else dies. It should be me."

His vision was blurred as he looked at Teddy who was still lying on the couch, staring at him curiously.

"Maybe if I had done this all those years ago, before it all started..." His voice broke as he shook his head. "None of this would have happened."

A sound caught his attention, an alert from his phone. Stepping away from the sharp object, he picked up the device and was greeted by a selfie from Cal. He was smiling; carefree, unaware of what was going through Shane's mind.

But seeing his face was enough. He couldn't touch those knives.

THE PHONE RANG AND HE GROANED AT THE THOUGHT OF answering it. It stopped ringing, and then started again, and again, until he couldn't stand the sound anymore.

"What?" he mumbled as he answered.

"Are you just waking up? It's after nine o'clock."

Of course. It was Callan, the last person he wanted to speak to. Not that he was in the mood to talk to anyone, except for Teddy, who only responded with barks and cuddles.

"I haven't had a stellar week." Sitting up slowly, he pressed a hand to his head.

"You didn't have a good Christmas?"

"No. I didn't go."

"Wait, you were alone for the holiday?" He paused. "Is everything okay? Is it your heart?"

Shane rolled his eyes. "Why are we playing twenty questions?"

"I assume you're not in the mood to talk about it then."

"No."

"Alright, I'll let it go." He sighed. "Are we still on for tonight?"

Shane had forgotten about their plans to get together after Christmas. The week had been a blur. He wasn't even sure what day of the week it was. The only thing he remembered doing was feeding Teddy and taking him outside when needed. "No. I can't."

"Oh, that's a shame. I was looking forward to your company."

"Cut the shit. I'm terrible company." Taking in a shuddering breath, he attempted to keep his voice steady. "No one should ever be around me."

"Shane, what's going on?"

"I can't talk right now."

"I'm coming over."

He planted his feet on the floor. If Callan stopped by, he didn't know that he'd be able to keep it together. "No, you can't."

"I know something's wrong, I can hear it in your voice."

Was there any point in trying to argue with him? It might be worse if he did. Cal, he could handle, but if he tried to come over with more people, or worse, the cops, Shane would lose control of the situation. "Fine."

There was another pause. "Is there anything you want to tell me?"

Gaze flicking to the sleeping dog on the floor, he licked his lips anxiously. "You want to know why there's a piece of Teddy's ear missing?"

"Okay."

"It's my fault. It's all my fault." His voice broke as curled back up on the couch. "Everything."

"Shane, you're not making sense." The sound of a car

door closing could be heard. "I'm on my way. You're at home?"

He sniffled. "Yeah."

"Don't go anywhere, alright? Just stay where you are."

Cal hung up and Shane heaved a sigh, wondering whether or not he had the physical strength to answer the door.

The amount of alcohol in his system would be enough to break down his walls. If Cal asked him any questions, he just might answer them truthfully.

He tried to think about how the conversation would go, what he should and shouldn't say. It was difficult to think when his mind was swimming with thoughts.

Before he was ready, there was a knock on the door, and Shane begrudgingly got up to open it.

He gave a half-hearted smile, gesturing for Cal to come inside. Shane closed the door with his foot and returned to his safe spot – the couch.

Teddy panted excitedly, wagging his tail as Cal leaned down to pet him. Then, pursing his lips, he stood in front of the curly-haired brunette.

"What's wrong, Shane? Tell me, please."

He shook his head.

Cal knelt in front of him. "You're not thinking about hurting yourself, are you?"

"What are you going to do, call the fucking cops?" Lying down on the couch, he turned on his side, face toward the cushions.

He sighed. "You're drunk."

"Yeah, you would be too if you were in my shoes."

"Is that safe with your medication?"

"Stop mothering me, for fuck's sake!" Looking over his

shoulder to see Teddy with his ears down, Shane instantly felt guilty. "Sorry, Teddy. I'm not mad at you, I promise."

"I'm worried about you." Cal placed a hand on his shoulder. "I can see that you're upset but I can't help you if you won't talk to me."

"Do you want to see my scars?" The words had come out of his mouth before he could stop them. For a moment, he wondered if Cal had even heard the offer because the room was silent.

"Shane, I..."

It could have been the alcohol talking, but if there was ever a time to show the love of his life the weight he carried with him, it was now. "Come on, I know you're curious about them." He sat up properly, though still facing the couch cushions instead of his boyfriend. "Wanna see what all the fuss is about?"

Callan heaved a sigh. "I don't want you to do this just because you're drunk. I know how sensitive of a subject this is for you."

"Do you want to see them or not?"

There was a long pause. Long enough that he almost fell asleep. And then came the answer.

"Okay, Shane. Okay."

He pulled the white t-shirt over his head and heard a soft gasp. Already, he was regretting the decision.

Shane felt brave enough to turn around and face the blond. Clearing his throat nervously, he tucked a curl behind his ear.

The color drained from Callan's face. His expression was beyond shock. Pursing his lips while the bottom one trembled, his tear-filled gaze examined each wound.

"My God, Shane. You were in this much pain?"

He shrugged and looked away, his heart racing from the

uncomfortable display. Other than his doctors, who had done nothing but shame him, this was the first time he'd been shirtless in front of anyone in a very long time. "Still am, I guess."

"It's okay, you don't have to hide from me. You're safe." Cal lifted Shane's chin, forcing him to look up. "Can I touch them?"

"Knock yourself out."

Callan took great care in his touch, fingers gently gliding over the various marks. Some were jagged, some were smooth, and most were in different directions across his skin, though a few of them overlapped.

He shook his head and quickly wiped away tears. "How did you get these? I know you couldn't have done all of this yourself."

Taking a deep breath, he placed a shaking hand over his chest, concentrating on the rapid beating of his heart and trying to slow it. "I like pain. You know that."

"Yes, but I don't think you liked these. The scars tell a story." Sitting on the couch, he leaned over to further examine Shane's back, his hand pressed against a few of the scars that connected. "They're angry. Your skin was torn. I don't think you wanted these. Your body wasn't prepared for them."

"Please stop," he whispered, head falling into his hands. "Stop asking about my scars. Just stop. I can't go down that road."

"Does that mean I'm onto something?"

"Cal, I mean it."

"If someone hurt you, they need to be held accountable."

"You don't understand!" His fingertips pressed into the edges of his face, knuckles turning white. "It was my father."

"Your...what?" Cal knelt in front of Shane once more, carefully prying his hands away from his face. "What did you say?"

He tried to take in several breaths but the air wouldn't reach his lungs. It was as if his body was rejecting the very idea of breathing; he couldn't manage it.

All the years of half-truths, lying by omission, and keeping the darkest secrets any child could keep against a parent, had finally caught up to him.

And it felt like dying. The cold air sweeping into his lungs seemed more like fire, his body shaking from the effort of remaining conscious.

"Shane, look at me, just breathe." Cal cupped the brunette's face in his hands. "I'm here. You're safe with me. Follow my breathing, alright? Try to match it."

Callan took in one breath after another and let each one out slowly. Shane did his best to follow suit while looking into those focused blue hues. Within a few minutes – although it seemed like forever – he was able to calm down.

Throwing his arms around Cal's neck, he held on tightly.

"You're the only person I've told," he confessed.

"I don't know what to say." His voice was just as strained as Shane's, but it sounded like he was trying to steady it. "I'm so sorry, Shane. I had no idea. But it all makes sense now."

"Just hold me, please."

Choking back a sob, Callan's arms slowly wrapped around him, hands pressed to bare skin. They stayed in each other's arms, both crying and attempting to dry one another's tears, but both sets of hands were damp from the effort and it was no use.

When he was ready, Shane pulled back and slipped his t-shirt back on. "There's another one, but I don't think..." Sniffling, he lifted up the edge of his shirt to wipe his face.

"It's my least favorite. I can't handle showing you that one."

"You don't have to." Cal placed a gentle kiss on his forehead. "I don't understand how you were able to keep this secret for so long. Has no one else questioned how you got those scars?"

"They bought my bullshit." He shrugged, hands resting between his knees. "I don't know if anyone thought it was strange, but they believed me. And my dad is just-he's really convincing. He taught me to be just as skilled in the art of lying. People will believe anything he says."

Furrowing his brow, he shook his head. "How did your family not know? Didn't they think it was suspicious that you came back from your father's house with new wounds?"

"I spent a lot of summers with him. That's mostly when it happened. The agreement was for six weeks out of every summer, but my mom was working a lot and didn't want me to be left to my own devices." Leaning back against the couch cushions, he pursed his lips. "Once she thought I was cutting myself, she insisted that I spend more time with my dad. So, he could, you know, keep an eye on me."

"Little did she know..." His bottom lip trembled. "Shane, I'm sorry. You've been in so much pain and I was blind to it."

"Don't cry for me, Cal. Please don't cry." Leaning forward, he ran a hand through Callan's hair. "You weren't blind to it. You knew something was wrong all along. I just couldn't tell you."

Clenching his jaw, he shot to his feet. "He's not going to get away with this. I won't let him."

"No, Cal, don't-" He took a tight hold of his hand. "Leave it alone. You don't know what he's like."

"I can *see* what he's like. He fucking tortured you!"

"I know, but, Cal..." Shane's voice was desperate as he

tried to find the right words. If anything happened to the man he loved, he would never forgive himself, and he was responsible for enough harm as it was. "If you say anything to him, or go after him, it won't matter. Nothing will come of it."

Callan's fists were clenched and his body was pointed in the direction of the door, but when he looked back at Shane, his fists loosened. "Maybe not tonight, but soon. I can't leave you like this."

"Well, you can't stay." Rubbing his tired eyes, he stood up, though he was swaying on his feet. "You shouldn't be here. You can't be around me, Cal. It's not safe."

"Why not?" He carefully wrapped his arms around Shane to keep him from falling. "Is this because you hit me? If it is, we'll work on it. You didn't mean it, Shane. You were coming out of a very serious nightmare and I don't blame you, okay? I can handle it."

Tears brimmed his eyes and he attempted to swallow the lump in his throat. "You shouldn't have to."

He placed a hand against Shane's cheek. "I will do anything to make this work."

"I'm really fucked up, Cal." Shaking his head, his fingers tapped his right temple. "I'm not right. My head is just...it's all fucked."

"I can't even imagine what you've been through, but you don't have to be alone. Let me take care of you."

One more night. That was all he wanted. One night where he had been vulnerable, one night where he had let his guard down, where he had fallen into utter despair and Callan had caught him.

Shane needed to know what that was like. Did it help? Did it validate everything he was saying? He already knew that it wasn't worth the risk, nothing was. No warm embrace, no tender kiss, and no words of comfort were worth someone's life.

But this was Callan. The moment they had laid eyes on one another, Shane had known that he would never want anyone else. When he had realized that he was in love with the tall blond, he had known that he would never love anyone else the way he loved Callan.

Would it be so terrible to allow himself one last night of comfort, to take Callan in, to feel the peace of being in his arms?

"Okay," he sighed in defeat. "You can stay, but you have to promise not to say anything to my father."

"For you? Anything."

Shane poked his chest. "I mean it, Cal. You have to promise."

"Alright, alright." Cal pulled him in closer. "I promise."

Even with the love of his life holding him close, Shane had another sleepless night. Cal began to stir. They laid there for some time, waiting for the sound of chirping birds before officially declaring themselves awake.

"How did you sleep?" Cal asked before pressing a kiss to his shoulder.

He was unaware that Shane had made several trips to the bathroom, his stomach trying to lurch contents that were non-existent. Hours of dry-heaving wasn't unusual given his situation. Sometimes it was the medication that produced the symptom. Other times, it was the memories.

"I didn't," he grumbled, throwing Cal's arm off him.

"You should have woken me. I would have stayed up with you."

With his feet planted on the floor and his back facing his lover, Shane buried his face in his hands. "You need to leave."

"Did I do something wrong?" He pressed a gentle hand to Shane's bare back. "Do you regret confiding in me?"

"Yes."

"Shane, I'll never tell a soul."

"I know."

"Then why do you regret it?"

"Because I regret *us*." Standing up to face the half-naked blond, he put his hands on his hips. "I regret meeting you. I regret letting you back into my life. I regret that I let you come here last night."

Sitting up in bed, Cal folded his arms. "You don't mean that."

"Are you calling me a liar again?"

Shaking his head, he averted his gaze. "Why are you doing this?"

He leaned down to pick up Cal's discarded clothing from the night before, throwing each individual item toward him. "Do you remember what you said to me the day you left?"

"Yes." His movements were slow as he pulled on his clothes, like a wounded animal afraid of further angering its owner. "I said that...we were never meant to last. That it would never work out between us."

"And?"

When he met Shane's gaze, his eyes were bloodshot and glossed over. "That our relationship was only temporary."

"That's what this was. That's what we always were. Temporary."

"Don't tell me that this is about some petty revenge." Getting out of bed, he gathered his socks and shoes, hastily putting them on. "I don't believe it. The things I've seen, what you've told me-"

"None of it matters!" He pinched the bridge of his nose, trying to find a tone within him that would sound convincing. "I don't want you, Cal. I thought I needed closure and I guess I have that now. We were never meant to last."

With a small nod, Cal walked down the hallway and Shane followed him. Seeing the hurt in his eyes made Shane want to take it all back immediately, but he needed to see this through.

"We're over. I don't want to see you again."

He stopped near the door, turning around and raising his hands as if to argue his point. But he seemed to think better of it, lowering his arms and shaking his head.

"This may be over for you, but it will never end for me. I will always love you, Shane."

"Don't do that to yourself." He opened the door and gestured for Cal to walk through it. "Move on. Go live your life."

Cal opened his mouth and closed it again. He was staring at the floor, gaze wandering between their feet and the cross of the threshold that would take him out of the apartment.

Shane could see that he was struggling to speak. He attempted to several times, but choked back sobs each instance. Shane gripped the door, knuckles white from the effort. It took every fiber of his being to focus on the bigger picture, to not throw his arms around Cal and comfort him.

It was better this way. As long as he remained stern, Cal would listen to him. But if he broke down, Cal would refuse to leave.

Finally, Cal took a deep breath, and spoke. "There is no life without you."

Rubbing his eyes to conceal the tears behind them, Shane shoved the tall blond over the threshold and closed the door in his face.

He could hear crying from the other side of the door.

Pressing his hand to the frame, he pursed his lips. It would have been so easy to open the door and welcome him back, but being near him was a death sentence.

Callan may never understand why Shane was breaking his heart, along with his own, but as long as Shane knew, that was all that mattered. The man's unconditional love for him would be his motivation. A reminder to keep it that way.

Boundaries were more important than love.

Safety was more important than love.

Callan's life was certainly worth more than the tightening in his chest, the palpitations, and the nausea sweeping over him.

Every light in the house was on. He could see it from the windows. Was it because she was afraid of the dark? Did the house seem infinitely lonelier without Ethan?

Taking a deep breath, he tapped the bottom of the door with his foot, hands full of presents.

The door opened and two small humans threw their arms around him.

"Uncle Shane!"

"Hi, guys!" His voice was higher than usual. Why was that? Was it guilt? What a stupid thing to do, as if a softer tone would ease the pain of their absent father. "Let me in, it's really cold out here."

Neither of them wanted to let go, both taking a hold of each arm, unconcerned about the gifts he was holding.

"Shane's here," Nora called out as she met him at the doorway. "Thanks for coming. I can help you with those."

She took a few of the gifts from him and then closed the door. "Are any of these for Ethan?"

He nodded slowly, now wondering if it had been a bad idea to bring them.

"We've kept his presents under the tree for when he comes home."

"Right."

Did she really believe that? She was a cop. The statistics were out there. As much as Shane hoped that his brother was alive somewhere, it was highly unlikely. Maybe Nora was clinging to hope because she needed to for the sake of the children.

Shane helped her set the gifts down, handing several to Harper and Hayden – somehow convincing them to let go of his arms before going into the kitchen to hug his mother.

"We missed you at Christmas," she whispered. "Where were you?"

"I was in bad shape," he muttered. "I would have ruined it for the twins."

Taking a step back, Lorraine looked him over. "How are you feeling? Have you been to the doctor lately?"

"I don't need to go to the doctor. I'm fine."

"Honey." She gave him a look. "You don't look well."

"Yeah, I'm f-" Quickly stopping himself from cursing, he cleared his throat. "I'm messed up and it shows."

"That's not what I mean and you know it."

Nora offered them both a mug of hot cocoa. Lorraine accepted and Shane politely declined. "Did I miss something?"

"Nope," he answered quickly, folding his arms.

"Uncle Shane, come sit with us!" Harper requested.

The adults were going to bore him anyway, so he didn't mind hanging out with his niece and nephew.

He sat on the couch, listening to the cartoons on the television while watching the twins open their gifts. They were so thankful for what little he'd managed to afford. He remembered being at that age and feeling that way over anything his mother bought for him; grateful for the smallest gift with the biggest effort.

Grimacing at the uncomfortable tightening of his chest, he rubbed it carefully, trying to make the sensation dissipate.

"Uncle Shane, will you read us a story?"

Gaze flicking to Hayden, he considered saying no and being on his way, but this may be the last time they were together. It wouldn't be fair to say no.

"Of course. Pick any one you want."

The two of them went over to the area where their books were stored and handed him what looked to be the largest one on the shelf.

He looked at them with his brow raised. "Really? This one?"

Harper nodded enthusiastically. "And you can't leave until you've read the whole thing to us."

Shane was about to comment on how long that would take him, and then realized that that was the very reason they had selected that particular book. They must not have wanted him to leave.

"Okay," he said softly. "How about...I'll stay until you fall asleep?"

"Fine," Hayden said with an exasperated sigh. "But not a minute sooner!"

Lorraine and Nora were occupied in the kitchen while Shane read what seemed to be the longest children's book he'd ever read. The kids even turned off the television just so that they could concentrate on the story.

With one twin snuggled in each arm, he couldn't hold

the book, and Harper and Hayden took turns with holding the book and turning the pages.

It took two hours for them to fall asleep, and Shane was true to his word. Before they had drifted off to the land of slumber, Harper had made him promise to return to read the rest of the story. It was a promise he knew that he wouldn't be able to keep, but with their pleading little faces, he couldn't have said no.

Lorraine took on the task of tucking them in while Shane and Nora were settled into an uncomfortable silence in the living room. The place wasn't really a mess but she insisted on cleaning it anyway.

"Do you need any help?" he asked.

"Not today. It would have been nice to have some on Christmas."

His breath hitched in his throat. He'd been waiting for her to make a comment. "Sorry."

"Do you know how much it would have meant to the kids to have you there on Christmas when Ethan couldn't be?" Her eyes were filled with tears, and she looked angry. "I know you don't give a shit about anyone except for yourself, but I thought you could at least pretend to care about the twins."

"I do care," he croaked, hand rubbing his chest again. "I just didn't think it would be good for them to see me so upset."

"Once again, it's all about you." Rolling her eyes, she snatched the book from his hand and returned it to the shelf. "Whatever helps you sleep at night."

"I don't sleep at night."

"Neither do I. Not anymore."

"I'm not like Ethan, okay? I don't know what you want from me."

"Don't you care that he's gone?" She approached him but kept her voice a harsh whisper, likely to prevent the twins from overhearing. "Those kids look at you like a father figure. It would be nice if you could stop being so goddamn selfish and step up to the plate." Her bottom lip trembled as she wiped away furious tears. "I think we both know Ethan's not coming back. The chances of a missing person being found decrease by the hour, and that's within the first two days."

"I know the statistics, Nora." He cleared his throat. "I know more than you think."

"Really? Do you know how much those kids love you? How much they *need* you?"

"Stop it," he pleaded, getting up from the couch. "I don't want to hear anymore."

"That's fine, Shane. I'm not going to tell them that you don't care, but one day, they'll figure it out for themselves."

"I can't be around them, Nora. They remind me too much of him."

"I want to know what it's like to be you," her voice broke. "To just wash your hands of everything, to never take responsibility."

"Don't say that." Raising his hand, he shook his head. "You have no idea what this is like."

She wiped her eyes again. "You lost a brother, but I lost my partner in life. I know you're in pain, but you can't possibly imagine how I feel."

"You're right, I don't, and I hope I never find out." Shane had to lean against the wall for support. "That's why I can't be around any of you. I don't want to hurt anyone."

Nora shook her head slowly. "You already have."

Bile was rising in his throat and he forced himself to swallow it, scrunching his nose as he did. "Goodbye, Nora."

Just as he turned to head for the door, his mother nearly walked into him.

"Sweetie, are you alright?" Lorraine pressed her palm to his forehead. "You look so pale. Are you having chest pains?"

"Mom, get off me. I mean it."

Lowering her hand, she frowned. "You're not leaving, are you?"

"I've been here for hours."

"But I haven't seen you since..." She took in a shuddering breath. "Please don't leave. I could use the company."

"No, I can't stay here and watch everyone cry, okay? I just can't deal with it." It was becoming increasingly difficult to breathe, neither of them were respecting his warnings, and it seemed like the walls were closing in on him. "Just leave me alone, you have to let me go."

"What do you mean?" Tears were streaming down her cheeks. "Shane, *please*, just talk to me."

Pushing past her, he made it out the door and retreated to the safety of his car. He took in one deep breath, and then another, trying to slow his heart rate.

"Fuck." He looked up at the house. There were significantly less lights on. "This is all so fucked."

Teddy, the only thing he couldn't distance himself from, was happy to see him walk through the door. He wagged his tail, giving Shane's face a few licks.

He took the dog outside, gave him a good brush, and then filled his food and water bowls.

Shane didn't feel like doing much these days, but he couldn't neglect Teddy. Not after everything they'd been through.

In a perfect world, he would have found a better home for his childhood pet. But someone had already given the poor aging boy away. And he wasn't going to let Teddy be abandoned for a third time.

They would be together until the end.

His cell-phone buzzed, signaling yet another missed call from Cal, accompanied by ones from Peter and his mother.

He might as well delete his contacts. There was no chance of reconnecting with them. This was it. He'd meant what he said.

With any luck, he would die in his sleep and that would be the end of it. They could hate him or mourn him, or both, but at least it would be over.

No more secrets.

No more lies.

And no justice either.

But, if nothing else, it would be over.

Groaning softly, he curled up on the couch, Teddy lying on the floor as close as he could be to his human. Shane rolled over to pet him absentmindedly as his mind wandered.

And the more it wandered, the more he realized the weight of it all. It was crushing him. That was why he couldn't seem to get enough air into his lungs.

The guilt, the pain, the gravity of his situation was too heavy to bear. His body was giving out under its weight.

Grabbing the pillow near his feet, Shane placed it in his lap before screaming into it.

April 3ʳᵈ 2010

Too much time had passed. There were so many rumors flying around – no one seemed to be taking Jake Talbot's disappearance seriously. Not even the police. What good were cops if they didn't go out there and find missing children?

The sad truth was that people didn't care anymore, they had moved on to the next tragedy, and the one after that. There was always something. Meanwhile, he and Missus Talbot were stuck in limbo.

Kids at school had a lot of useless theories – that Jake had run away because he was miserable at home, that he'd gotten a girl pregnant (which was absolutely ridiculous because everyone knew that he was gay), or that he was on drugs somewhere – none of which made a lick of sense to Shane.

They had been close until his disappearance, as close as he would allow himself to get to a person. Maybe he didn't know Jake as well as he'd thought. Maybe he had run away, and maybe Shane was the reason.

"What do you want for your birthday dinner?" his father grumbled from the front seat.

Shane shrugged as he looked out of the car window. "Whatever you want, I guess, it doesn't matter to me."

"It's not my birthday."

"Like you care," he muttered.

"What did you say?" Unsurprisingly, his father's voice had risen.

He slouched in the back seat. "Nothing, sir."

Their route home was like a stroll down memory lane. They passed Jake's favorite restaurant, their school, the street where Jake had lived. It made him furrow his brow, almost as if his father knew how much he was thinking about the boy today. Was it a way of showing that he cared, or was he trying to be a jerk?

Leaning against the car door as they passed the park where he'd last seen Jake, he heaved a sigh. The posters stapled onto trees were faded. Poor Missus Talbot had to keep taking the old ones down and putting fresh ones up. They all read the same thing:

Missing:
Jacob Talbot
Birth Date: March 9th, 1995
Date Missing: January 31st, 2010
Description: White, medium build, short brown hair, green eyes, last seen wearing a red hoodie and blue jeans

Shane wondered if the red hoodie Jake had been wearing was the same one that he'd made Shane sign on the tag. Jake had been convinced that Shane would be a famous author one day and had wanted a wearable autograph.

He tried to wipe his eyes carefully so that his father wouldn't see, but the older man was watching him in the rear view mirror. "Shame about that boy."

That was odd. Shane's father had never commented on the subject before. Of course he knew that Jake had gone missing, they lived in the same neighborhood, so how could he not? But they had never discussed his friend's disappearance.

He thought about what would have happened if he'd never met Jake. Would Shane have met someone else – someone better, someone worse?

If he and Jake had never met, would he still have gone missing? He couldn't imagine his first crush, or his first boyfriend, being anyone else.

"Yeah," he spoke quietly. "Everyone misses him."

There was a long, uncomfortable silence. It was something he'd grown accustomed to. This one seemed different, like his father was waiting for something. There was tension in the air. Perhaps because his father knew that he and Jake had been a thing – something – whatever they had been. His father was probably glad that the boy had gone missing. That wouldn't have surprised him.

So, what was it this time? What was he waiting for – an

admission? An apology? Well, he wasn't going to get either of those things. Shane wasn't sorry for having a relationship with Jake.

Finally, his father's voice broke the silence. "They'll never find that faggot's body."

Every bit of air was pulled from his lungs. Most people might have assumed that his father was just being insensitive, but Shane knew that it was more than that.

They stopped at a red light, Shane still hesitant to take a breath as his gaze met his father's in the rear view mirror. There was a look in the man's eyes, something like pride, which to him said, this means exactly what you think it means.

The air flooded back into his lungs but he still couldn't breathe. He rolled down his window for extra oxygen, beads of sweat forming on his brow.

His heart was racing.

His stomach was churning.

This wasn't happening. It couldn't be.

Because if it was, it meant that his father was a murderer. If it was, it meant that Jake was dead. If it was, it meant that his father had killed Jake because of him.

13

Someone's fist was pounding on his door.

Someone was calling his name.

"Go away!" he shouted at them, not wanting the ruckus to disturb the neighbors. The last thing he needed was the cops at his doorstep.

"Good to know you're alive, kid."

The voice belonged to Peter.

"Why don't you answer your phone, Shane? I thought you were dead."

"Wishful thinking."

Knowing that if he didn't allow the man inside it would make matters worse, he begrudgingly opened the door before returning to the couch.

Nausea was clouding his judgment as he pulled a blanket over his face.

"Kid, what the hell is this?"

The blanket was peeled back to reveal a sickeningly pale Shane. Peter reached out to touch him but then pulled back, as if he thought touching the frail young man would cause him to shatter.

"You're in bad shape," he spoke in a low voice. "You need to see a doctor."

"I'm fine," Shane stressed, though he most certainly was not.

"Come on, get up. We're leaving right now."

As soon as the man's hand gripped his arm, Shane smacked it away. "Stay away from me!"

Peter furrowed his brow, apparently alarmed by the physical contact. "Why?"

"Because you shouldn't be helping me." He took a deep breath, tears escaping from his eyelids as he closed them. "Not when I didn't help *you*."

"What are you talking about, kid?"

"I know what happened to your son. It's my fault...it's all my fault."

He paused, his expression changing from one of concern to one of shock. "You knew Jake?"

"Yeah, I did." Shane swallowed hard. "But I didn't know that the kid I knew was your son until I went to your house."

"That's why you were acting so strangely." Realization seemed to meet him like a tidal wave as his face twisted in anger. "Shane, what happened to my son?"

He immediately averted his gaze. "I-I can't tell you."

"Did you do something to him?"

"No, I didn't-" He raised his hands defensively. "I wouldn't-"

Shane was pulled to his feet, Peter roughly holding him up by the collar of his shirt. "Tell me what happened!"

With a whimper, he covered his face with his hands. Peter released Shane as tears soaked his palms and he slid to the floor. He rocked back and forth, each gasping breath quickening the beat of his heart. Shane curled into a ball in an attempt to lessen the shaking of his body, but it didn't work.

Peter must have realized that he wasn't going to get a straight answer out of Shane because he knelt beside him, placing a hand on his shoulder.

"Let's get you some help. And then you can tell me all about it."

"Just leave me," Shane cried. "No matter what I do, this will end badly."

He shook his head. "I'm not going to go away. I'm leaving now, but I'll be back. I won't rest until I find out what happened to Jake."

"I know." Shane wiped his eyes. "You're a good father. I wish you were mine."

Tension hung in the air, almost as thick as the eerie silence. The only thing that broke them from it was Teddy's soft whining.

"What the fuck is going on here, kid? I can't figure you out."

"Good. Now get out." Making his way to the cowering dog, Shane wrapped his arms around him. "Leave us alone."

Although his fists were clenched, Peter did so without another word.

He'd never seen the man so angry. It made him wonder what would happen if he told the truth. Nothing – and no one – was a match for Victor Gray. He had learned that the hard way, and he'd be damned if anyone else he cared about had to learn that lesson.

No one else could disappear on his watch.

The police would feign ignorance.

The public would be at a loss for knowledge.

Shane Coulter knew the truth, and it would die with

him. Because if it didn't, everyone he loved would be in danger.

MAYBE HE HAD BEEN TOO HARSH WITH HIS MOTHER. IF SHE disappeared, Victor would be the first suspect. He couldn't possibly be that stupid, so maybe she was safe from his father's wrath for that very reason.

At the very least, she deserved a heartfelt goodbye, not a rushed and angry one.

Knocking softly on the door, he took a step back and warmed his hands in the pockets of his coat.

The person who answered the door was someone he knew all too well and the last person he'd expected.

"Peter?" The older man simply stared at him, not saying a word. "What the fuck? Why are you answering my mother's door?"

Pushing Peter aside, Lorraine offered an apologetic smile. "Shane, honey, we wanted to tell you..."

His gaze narrowed, moving from one to the other. He wasn't sure what he was feeling. Betrayal? Anger? Relief?

Peter was a good man, and he knew that his mother would be treated well, but he had to wonder how long they'd been seeing one another.

"So *that's* why you started giving a shit about me." He nodded slowly. "You were seeing my mom."

Peter sighed. "That's not why."

"Oh, really? I'm supposed to believe that you suddenly caring about me and my life isn't connected to you trying to score points with my mother?"

His jaw was clenched and he pointed at Shane's chest. "You don't get to be angry about this. If memory serves, you've kept a number of secrets yourself."

"I bet you've told her all about them, haven't you?" He scoffed. "I can never trust you, either of you, because whatever I say isn't private."

Lorraine got between them. "Shane, sweetie, we both love you. We're not talking behind your back, we're just worried about you."

"Whatever." Trotting down the porch steps, he walked back toward his car. "I'm done."

Peter followed him, blocking the driver's side door. "You were just looking for an excuse to cut us out of your life."

"Yeah, and now you've given me one. Congratulations." His gaze flicked toward his mother. "You've made this a hell of a lot easier on me."

"How convenient for you." Peter leaned in closer, forcing Shane to look at him. "The only reason I'm taking it easy on you is because of *her*. Count yourself lucky. A parent will do anything to protect their child."

"I wouldn't know." He shoved Peter out of the way and opened the car door. "I hope you get your answers someday, but I can't be the one to give them to you."

"So...you *do* know what happened to him."

Shane placed his hand on the door handle, ready to close it. "Haven't you learned to take everything I say with a grain of salt? It's all bullshit."

"Get the fuck out of here," he sneered. "Before I regret letting you walk away."

Slamming the door, Shane wasted no time in starting the vehicle and pulling out of the driveway.

It was all going according to plan. He had successfully pushed everyone away.

That didn't make the sting any less painful.

. . .

HIS BREATHING WAS HEAVY, HEART POUNDING AGAINST HIS ribcage. He didn't have to do this. There was no need for confirmation. Deep down, he already knew. The minute his brother had gone missing, he had known who was responsible. This was just a formality.

So why was he here? Maybe he *did* need that confirmation, the kind that Peter and Missus Talbot never had. He had to know for sure what had happened.

There was no way in Hell that he was going to that man's house. Shane was many things, but he wasn't stupid. There was no telling if he'd ever come out of it again, and that would have been on *him* because he'd entered knowing – or suspecting – what had occurred there.

Swallowing hard, he opened the door to the small cafe and walked inside. The place was empty except for what he assumed was the chef; he could hear the clanking of pans and sizzling of a fryer. He couldn't help but wonder if his father had done this on purpose, renting out the place to ensure privacy. Though, perhaps that was his paranoia talking. Paranoia that his father had created. Paranoia that had been proven correct countless times.

His heart was racing as he sat across from his abuser. Victor Gray. Captain Victor Gray, formally Detective Victor Gray. The usual smug, twisted smirk was on his father's face.

"It's good to see you, son. How long has it been?"

There was an involuntary pause because he was having difficulty getting words to come out of his mouth. "S-six years."

"You cast me aside the moment you turned eighteen." He clicked his tongue. "That was hurtful."

"To your reputation, maybe." He folded his arms. "You never gave a shit about me."

"How can you say that when I've put so much effort into making you the way you are?"

Shane's jaw clenched. Is that what this was – amusement? A game? To the twisted mind, it must have seemed perfectly natural, but Shane had never been able to wrap *his* mind around it. Torture for pleasure. Murder for fun. It made his stomach churn. "You wanted to leave your mark. Mission fucking accomplished."

"Not exactly. I wanted you to be so much more." Victor shook his head slowly. "Don't ever have children, Shane. They will only disappoint you."

He opened his mouth to speak, but an elderly man emerged from the kitchen doors. It made him even more nervous because it wasn't just *his* safety at stake.

Victor ordered a full meal and Shane, hesitantly, ordered coffee.

"Not hungry?" Victor asked with a slight smile.

"Lost my appetite." His gaze shifted to the man's waist – his jacket was open just enough to show off his badge and gun. "They haven't kicked you out yet?"

"On the contrary." Victor took a sip of black coffee before continuing. "I'm up for promotion. The people love me, Shane. They can't understand why you don't."

It was bullshit. All of it. Everything. There were numerous times when he'd asked for help, but no one had believed him; they'd known and hadn't cared. Someone always knew. They just pretended not to. "Why can't they see you for what you are?"

"They are the blind leading the blind. And those who *can* see choose not to. People don't like to accept the truth when it's ugly."

His father was using that prideful tone. He was pleased with his accomplishments and enjoyed every bit of it. Shane had never been the only one who could see Victor for what he was, he was certain of that. But he was the only one who *challenged* him. And maybe that was the reason for all of this. It was possible that his father also enjoyed being challenged, this little game of cat and mouse. That may have been why Shane was still alive knowing what he knew.

"Why do you have to include me in your sordid fucking life?" he asked through gritted teeth. "Why do you keep torturing me?"

"Because you make it so easy."

Shane's gaze wandered to the kitchen doors. "Should we be talking about this with the cook in the back?"

"He's hard of hearing. But don't worry," Victor lowered his voice, "I brought enough bullets for both of you."

Shane chewed the inside of his lip, contemplating his next move. Fight or flight. Sink or swim. What would be the smarter thing to do? His nostrils flared, giving away the anger he was trying to conceal. It wouldn't do him any good. His father had too much strength, too much power. "I thought that if I remained silent, you'd leave me alone."

"Well, I did, didn't I?"

"So, why now?"

"Because you're my finale." The cook served the food and once again disappeared behind the kitchen doors. Victor continued speaking as if it were the average conversation. "I'm not as young as I once was. There will come a time when I'm not physically able to do certain things no matter how much I want to."

"*Certain things*? You mean *kill* people." The twinkle in his father's eye sent chills down his spine. He couldn't stay there much longer; his heart couldn't take it. The only thing left to do was ask the question. "How many others are there besides Jake Talbot?"

"I'm not going to tell you that." Victor tilted his head. "That would take away the thrill of the mystery."

Closing his eyes to mask his tears, he turned away, facing the window. "You once told me that you wished I could have been more like Ethan, that you would rather have him for a son than me. I thought you liked him."

"I did. I do." He paused. "I always will."

"Then why?" he whispered, unable to muster anything above that volume.

"Why *what*, Shane?" The corners of his lips were twitching. Clearly, he wanted Shane to say the words.

"Why is he missing?"

"You already know the answer to that. Otherwise, we wouldn't be here, and you wouldn't have asked."

"I kept my word," Shane said breathlessly. "I never told anyone."

Victor's gaze wandered over his son before he returned his attention to his meal. "I believe you."

Thank God for that – because he was lying. Not that telling people had accomplished anything.

He shook his head slowly, brow furrowed. "Then why did you take my brother?"

"You wouldn't see me, Shane." His father's tone was flippant as if the young man shouldn't have expected anything less. "How else was I supposed to get your attention?"

Two people were dead because of him. Shane had to wonder if there was anyone else connected to him that had gone missing; old teachers, past friends, distant relatives he'd never met, acquaintances who had been unlucky enough to say hello to him.

His father could take anyone at any time, for any reason or no reason at all. And it was because he enjoyed it. That, and he liked watching Shane squirm.

Despite the hopelessness and despair he felt, he wouldn't allow Victor to see any of it.

"Fuck you."

He left the restaurant, got into his car, and drove for as long as he could stand it. Then, when he was certain that he hadn't been followed, Shane parked on the side of the road. His knuckles were white as he gripped the steering wheel.

For years, he had thought his silence had bought him time and protection. After all, doing the opposite had been pointless. When people said things that sounded as though it could only be a work of fiction, most assumed that it was. And those who didn't could end up dead.

Yet, Jake hadn't known a thing. Neither had Ethan. So, had his silence really protected them? Had it all been worth it?

There could be no victory in this, no happy ending. Even if his father finally got what he deserved, it wouldn't replace what Shane had lost or what he stood to lose.

His hands fell from the wheel as he brought them to his face and cried all the tears he refused to let his father see. The hole inside him was so vast that it felt as though his chest had caved in. His breaths sounded more like gasps, lungs trying to swoop in the air as he struggled to satisfy them.

His body was shaking so violently that he had to climb into the back seat and curl up to contain it. With his eyes closed and sobs racking his slender frame, Shane wondered how he was going to survive with this incurable devastation.

WHY COULDN'T THEY STOP CALLING? HADN'T HE DONE enough to render himself irredeemable? Apparently not. If they needed him to add more fuel to the fire, he could do that.

With one hand rubbing his chest, he answered his phone with the other.

"Did I not make myself clear?"

There was a long pause. And it took everything in him not to beg Callan to say something. Shane missed hearing his voice. His other half would never know it, but Callan was the air he breathed. Without him, Shane would wither and die. But it was a price he was willing to pay. Cal wasn't safe with him.

"Why didn't you tell me about your brother?"

A sigh of relief, though he hoped it came across as exasperation. "It wouldn't have mattered."

"I'm a journalist, Shane." His voice was shaky. "You know that I've spoken to your family, and...and Pete."

Fuck. He should have known this was coming. "So what?"

"You keep saying that everything is your fault."

"Yeah. I don't know why people never believe me."

"I'm starting to. I'm trying to understand."

"Understand what, Cal?" Was this part going according to plan too? Had he set enough clues, planted enough seeds? "Go on. Just say what you're thinking."

"You said that you're the reason Teddy's missing a part of his ear."

It was okay that Callan believed that because he and Teddy knew the truth. The poor dog was just another victim of his father.

"Yep," he lied.

"And you knew Jake Talbot. Peter said you made some comments to him about the boy's disappearance."

"Uh-huh."

"Now Ethan is missing and...you're taking responsibility for that too."

"And?"

Callan took a deep breath. "Did you hurt them? Are you the reason they're missing?"

Bingo. That was exactly what Shane needed him to think. He may have been close, but as long as Cal wasn't directly on Victor's trail, he might be safe. "I don't think we should be talking about this."

There was a very long pause. "Talk to me, Shane. *Please.* If you're sick, we can get you help. You might have some alternate personality who's making you do these things. It's not your fault, you can't help it. These things happen sometimes when a person has suffered severe trauma. And, Shane, you've been through so much. Let me help you."

An alternate personality, huh? That was original. It didn't matter what Cal believed as long as he believed that Shane was responsible for all of it. "Write your story, Cal. Do whatever you want to do. Just don't contact me again."

"Wait, Sha-"

He hung up the phone and slammed it down. It would all be worth it in the end. That was how he lived with the agony. The pain in his chest might grow, and his heart might beat right out of his chest, but at least his loved ones would be safe. For now.

Looking over at Teddy, who was peering at him quizzically, he nodded slowly. "Cal thinks I cut your ear off. I let him believe that. Do you remember when my dad did that to you?"

Teddy walked over to him as if Shane was offering a treat.

"Yeah, I bet you do. So do I." Pursing his lips, he scratched behind the dog's ears. "That was when I knew that I wouldn't be able to keep you. Or anyone, for that matter."

If he was to be Victor's finale, he had to assume that people were going to get hurt somewhere between here and the finish line. He didn't know how, but he had to find some way to end it.

If Victor was intent on making him suffer, Shane could see no other alternative than taking matters into his own hands.

Victor might not harm the people he loved if Shane himself was no longer there to torture.

As if Teddy had figured out his thought process, he whined and pawed Shane's lap.

"Sorry, boy. It might be the only way." He delivered a kiss to the dog's head. "But I won't make my decision until you're gone. I promised I wouldn't abandon you again."

Tomorrow, he could create a mental plan for what was to come. The day after, he could ensure its possibility.

Tonight, he was going to sit with his dog and mull over his options. There weren't many at his disposal. He only saw one way out of this, but there was no guarantee that his untimely death would stop the murders. And if he was dead, there was no way of knowing whether or not that plan had been a success.

What if it had the opposite effect and Victor was left unsatisfied?

One way or another, this was all going to end in his demise. The only thing up for debate was whether or not others died with him, for him, or because of him.

"We're the only two living creatures on earth who know the truth." Shane wrapped his arms around Teddy. "That means we have to decide what to do with that knowledge. One way or another, people are going to die, Teddy. I just hope it's me. And Victor."

Lowering his arms as well as his face, he closed his eyes. "Or even just me...if it spares the others."

ABOUT THE AUTHOR

Laurencia Hoffman specializes in various sub-genres of romance. Her stories often focus on the darker side of fiction, but love and survival remain the central themes throughout her work.

When she's not writing, she also enjoys playing video games with her family, listening to music, satisfying her sweet tooth, and watching films.